wawiyatācimowinisa

ᐘᐏᔭᑖᒋᒧᐏᓂᓴ

Funny Little Stories

wawiyatācimowinisa

ᐊᐧᐃᐧᔭᑖᒋᒧᐃᐧᓂᓴ

Funny Little Stories

Narrated by Cree-speaking students, instructors and Elders
Transcribed and translated by Cree Linguistics students
Edited and with a Glossary and Syllabics by Arok Wolvengrey

Memoir 1
First Nations Language Readers

First Nations University of Canada
and
Canadian Plains Research Center

2007

UNIVERSITY OF REGINA

CANADIAN PLAINS RESEARCH CENTER

FIRST NATIONS UNIVERSITY OF CANADA

Library and Archives Canada Cataloguing in Publication
wawiyatācimowinisa = funny little stories / narrated by Cree-speaking students, instructors and elders ; transcribed and translated by Cree linguistics students ; edited and with a glossary and syllabics by Arok Wolvengrey.

(University of Regina publications, ISSN 1480-000; no. 17)
Text in Cree and English.
Cree syllabics also appears in title information.
Includes bibliographical references.
ISBN 978-0-88977-185-7

1. Cree language--Readers. I. Wolvengrey, Arok, 1965- II. University of Regina. Canadian Plains Research Center. III. Series.

PM989.W39 2007 497'.3
C2007-901692-8

We acknowledge the financial support of the Government of Canada through the Book Publishing Industry Development Program (BPDIP) for our publishing activities. We acknowledge the support of the Canada Council for the Arts for our publishing program.

Cover design: Brian Danchuk Design, Regina
Printed and bound in Canada by Houghton Boston, Saskatoon.

*Note: All royalties from the sale of this book, above and beyond recovering the cost of production, revert to the First Nations Language Readers Fund to support the further production of volumes in this series. The stories recounted herein remain the intellectual property of their creators.

The artwork contained in this volume was produced by Melissa Sanderson, a 14 year old Cree youth from Opāskwēyāk Cree Nation, presently residing in Regina and attending high school at Balfour Collegiate. Melissa has been creating art since she was four years old and has won awards in competitions in and around Regina.

Contents

Foreword

This collection of short Cree stories is the first volume in a new series of First Nations language readers. As the first of the series, it serves as a sampler of stories from different genres, different generations and different dialects. Future volumes will each present stories in one of the languages of the Canadian prairies, sometimes built around a common theme, sometimes simply representing a range of topics and/or genres in a particular language. And occasionally, a common theme will allow us to cross language boundaries in a collection of stories from a number of First Nations languages.

With regard to the present volume, I am grateful to all those who participated in the gathering of these texts. Many were collected by students participating in Cree language courses at the First Nations University of Canada (formerly SIFC), whether narrating their own stories or interviewing others. I am particularly grateful to those Elders and teachers who narrated stories for the students' use, and to the family of Mary Louise Rockthunder for permission to include the final text herein. Our Elder Mary Louise has since passed to the spirit world, but we hope this first published offering of her humour will stand as testament of her skill and wit in storytelling.

Much of the inspiration for this volume and the entire series comes from a number of Cree scholars and/or scholars specializing in Cree. First and foremost is Dr. Freda Ahenakew who, as instructor, mentor, colleague, *ēkwa mīna ē-oyokāwīsiyān*, has meant so much to me and first encouraged me to work with the Cree language. Following Freda from Saskatchewan to Winnipeg allowed me to study under and work with Dr. H.C. Wolfart, whose years of experience with Cree provided me with the best possible linguistic training. The influence of Drs. Ahenakew and Wolfart can also be seen in the format of this volume, which closely follows the first of Freda's publications, *kiskinahamawākan-ācimowinisa*, presented by Algonquian and Iroquioan Linguistics under Dr. Wolfart's editorship. The training I received from these two led me to my current position at the First Nations University of Canada where I have had the privilege to work with many wonderful colleagues and students in the Department of Indian Languages, Literatures, and Linguistics. In the context of this current volume, there are two in particular to whom I owe special thanks. Solomon Ratt has been there for me from my first interview for my current position, through Cree language immersion camps and Cree language retention committee meetings, as colleague, boss, and friend. I am extremely grateful for all of his guidance and especially for his co-operation in serving as a consultant for one of my students and his permission to have his story printed herein. Finally, I will never be able to adequately express my gratitude to my colleague, friend and partner, Dr. Jean Okimāsis, for the abiding inspiration she provides.

kinanāskomitināwāw kahkiýaw

Arok Wolvengrey
September, 2007

Introduction

This is the first in a series of readers in the First Nations languages of the prairie provinces meant for language learners and language users. The stories in this volume come from a variety of sources, all being narrated or written by fluent speakers of Cree, whether students or instructors of the Cree language or Elders, and representing a wide array of dialect differences including examples of Plains, Woods and Swampy Cree. Once narrated and recorded, these stories were then transcribed in the Standard Roman Orthography (SRO) for Cree—and translated into English—by students in the Cree Linguistics and Cree Language Studies programs at the First Nations University of Canada (formerly known as the Saskatchewan Indian Federated College). Ultimately, all stories were given a final edit for SRO spelling, transliterated into Syllabics and organized into glossaries by the volume editor. Additionally, a title page has been provided for each text which gives further information on the source of each text and the path it took to the published page.

The nine stories that comprise this volume can be read in three sets of three, each set representing a different genre of Cree story. The first three very short stories are essentially jokes based on wordplay and the contact of Cree and English culture and language, each narrated/written by a fluent speaker of Plains Cree enrolled in the Cree Language Studies program: Guy Albert of Sandy Lake (*ýēkawiskāwikamāhk*) on Ahtahkakoop (*atāhkakohp*) First Nation, Doreen Martell of Waterhen Lake (*sihkihp-sākahikan*) First Nation, and Neil Sapp of Little Pine First Nation (*wāskicōsiýinīnāhk*).

The second set of three stories are humorous accounts of life experiences in a variety of settings, as told by student, teacher and Elder respectively. Bealiqué Kahmahkotayo, a student from Little Pine First Nation, told of a favourite family memory. Solomon Ratt, a professor in the Department of Indian Languages, Literatures, and Linguistics at the First Nations University, originally hailing from the Woods Cree community of Stanley Mission (*āmaciwīspimowinihk*), narrated a bittersweet reminiscence from his own residential school experience. He was recorded by Jacyntha Laviolette, a student in the Linguistics program and a non-speaker of Cree who bravely took on the daunting task of attempting to transcribe and translate a language (and dialect) largely unfamiliar to her. Another student in the Cree Language Studies program, Delbert Alexson of Starblanket First Nation, made a similar contribution by recording Elder Gilbert Starr. Elder Starr is, in fact, the grandson of *acāhkosa k-ōtakohpit* ("he who has stars as a blanket"), for whom the Starblanket First Nation is named. Elder Starr recounted two stories of a traditional trapping lifestyle originally told by his father and his uncle.

The third set of tales are traditional stories (*ātaýōhkēwina*) of the Trickster-Hero, Wīsahkēcāhk. The first one is told by speakers of Swampy Cree from Moose Lake (*mōs-sākahikan*) First Nation, Manitoba. Wilfred James Martin narrated a story for his sister Vivian Young, a graduate student at First Nations University, who re-recorded, transcribed and translated it. For the second text, another student from Moose Lake, Jeff Sanderson, recorded his mother, Annabelle, telling a whole cycle of Wīsahkēcāhk tales and we offer this first one here. The final *ātaýōhkēwin* and the last story in this collection is the only one not recorded as part of a University assignment. Elder Mary Louise Rockthunder of Piapot First Nation (*nēhiýaw-pwātināhk*) told this hilarious story of Wīsahkēcāhk to the great amusement of all in attendance at a 2001 teachers' workshop organized by the Saskatchewan Cree Language Retention Committee, and it is offered here in her memory.

As mentioned above, the formal presentation of these texts and the vocabulary from them is organized into three main sections, and each deserves some further introduction. In turn below, the sections including the Cree Syllabics, the Cree Standard Roman Orthography (SRO) and English translation, and the Cree-English Glossary will be described.

Cree Syllabics

In the first section, ᐊᐧᐃᐧᔭᑖᒋᒧᐃᐧᓂᓴ, all texts are given in Cree Syllabics. For all but one text, this means the standard Western Cree Syllabary is used, including all appropriate conventions such as the overposed dot indicating vowel length (e.g. ᐸ = pa; ᐹ = pā), the final for "h" (ᐦ) indicating pre-aspiration, and a following dot indicating a pre-vocalic "w" (e.g. ᐊ = a; ᐊᐧ = wa; ᐯ = pē; ᐯᐧ = pwē). The Syllabic chart in Figure 1 (on the following page) illustrates this standard Western Cree Syllabary.

The one exceptional Syllabics text is text 5 which is narrated in the "th" dialect or Woods Cree. Though Woods Cree can be written using the standard Syllabary, two important modifications have been incorporated into a Syllabary specific to the needs of the Woods Cree dialect. The first, a requirement for any syllabic system to fully represent the sounds of Woods Cree, is the addition of a symbol for the "th" (or /ð/) sound. The row containing the variants of this symbol (e.g. ᖬ = tha)

Figure 1
Western Cree Syllabary (Plains and Swampy Cree)

	ē	i	o	a	ī	ō	ā	
	ᐁ	ᐃ	ᐅ	ᐊ	ᐄ	ᐆ	ᐋ	finals
w	ᐁ·	ᐃ·	ᐅ·	ᐊ·	ᐄ·	ᐆ·	ᐋ·	ᐤ
p	ᐯ	ᐱ	ᐳ	ᐸ	ᐲ	ᐴ	ᐹ	ᑊ
t	ᑌ	ᑎ	ᑐ	ᑕ	ᑏ	ᑑ	ᑖ	ᐟ
k	ᑫ	ᑭ	ᑯ	ᑲ	ᑮ	ᑰ	ᑳ	ᐠ
c	ᒉ	ᒋ	ᒍ	ᒐ	ᒌ	ᒎ	ᒑ	ᐨ
m	ᒣ	ᒥ	ᒧ	ᒪ	ᒦ	ᒨ	ᒫ	ᒼ
n	ᓀ	ᓂ	ᓄ	ᓇ	ᓃ	ᓅ	ᓈ	ᐣ
s	ᓭ	ᓯ	ᓱ	ᓴ	ᓰ	ᓲ	ᓵ	ᐢ
y	ᔦ	ᔨ	ᔪ	ᔭ	ᔩ	ᔫ	ᔮ	ᐩ

l ᓬ	r ᕒ	h ᐦ	hk ᕁ

Figure 2
Woods Cree Syllabary

	ī	i	o	a	ō	ā	
	ᐁ	ᐃ	ᐅ	ᐊ	ᐆ	ᐋ	finals
w	ᐍ	ᐏ	ᐓ	ᐘ	ᐕ	ᐚ	ᐤ
p	ᐯ	ᐱ	ᐳ	ᐸ	ᐴ	ᐹ	ᑊ
t	ᑌ	ᑎ	ᑐ	ᑕ	ᑑ	ᑖ	ᐟ
k	ᑫ	ᑭ	ᑯ	ᑲ	ᑰ	ᑳ	ᐠ
c	ᒉ	ᒋ	ᒍ	ᒐ	ᒎ	ᒑ	ᐨ
m	ᒣ	ᒥ	ᒧ	ᒪ	ᒨ	ᒫ	ᒼ
n	ᓀ	ᓂ	ᓄ	ᓇ	ᓅ	ᓈ	ᐣ
s	ᓭ	ᓯ	ᓱ	ᓴ	ᓲ	ᓵ	ᐢ
y	ᔦ	ᔨ	ᔪ	ᔭ	ᔫ	ᔮ	ᐩ
th	ᖧ	ᖨ	ᖪ	ᖬ	ᖫ	ᖭ	ᙾ

l ᓬ	r ᕒ	h ᐦ	hk ᕽ

is simply added as the last line in Figure 2 (on the preceding page) illustrating the Woods Cree Syllabary. Figure 2 also includes a significant difference from the Western Cree Syllabary in Figure 1. Due to a sound shift in Woods Cree, no symbol is required for the vowel /ē/ found in both Plains and Swampy Cree. As such, the syllabic symbols normally used for /ē/ are instead used for the vowel /ī/ in Woods Cree. This reduces the number of columns needed in the Woods Cree Syllabary by one, as the original /ī/ series (with overposed dot) is no longer needed.

In practical terms, the Woods Cree Syllabary is sufficient to represent the Woods Cree dialect, and readers of other dialects need only remember that the /ē/ series is to be read as /ī/ for Woods Cree. This may take some getting used to, as the symbols used for this sound will match /ē/ for Plains and Swampy Cree, leading to the appearance of an overabundance of /ē/ syllables. Sometimes this correspondence works well.

For instance, the symbol ᐯ can be read as *pē-* in Plains and Swampy Cree and as *pī-* in Woods Cree, each meaning "come towards" as appropriate in each dialect. Similarly, the spelling ᒣᑕᐌ will correspond with Plains and Swampy *mētawē* and Woods Cree *mītawī*, both meaning "play." However, in other cases, a Woods Cree word will not convert to the appropriate Plains or Swampy form. For instance, the Woods Cree spelling ᑫᐌ (*kīwī* "go home"), would seem to correspond with Plains and Swampy "kēwē," when in fact the appropriate form for both of those dialects is *kīwē*. Therefore, it is important to know which dialect, and thus which Syllabary, is being represented in any given text. As already mentioned, only text 5 of the current volume uses this modified Woods Cree Syllabary.

Special note must also be made of some additional symbols that are found in the Syllabic texts. For the most part, this involves punctuation, such as commas, semi-colons, colons, periods, exclamation marks and questions marks, which match the punctuation from the SRO representation of Cree. English words found in the Cree texts are simply presented in the regular English spelling (in italics), and no attempt has been made to translate or otherwise present the words in either Cree orthography. Finally, quotations are opened and closed by double pointed brackets (« ») or *les guillemets* in French punctuation, though their use here follows English rather than French practice and corresponds directly to quotations as represented in the SRO texts. On occasion one quotation is embedded within another. In such cases the pointed brackets are used for both levels of quotation, but the quote within a quote is given in italicized print, as in this example from text number 6.

« « *ᓂᑖᐸᑿᒪᐚᐤ ᐊᓄᐦᐨ ᐊᐘ ᑳ ᑳᐦ ᑭᑐᑕᒪᐏᐟ*
ᓯᐦᑯᐢ,» ᓂᑕᐩ ᐃᑖᐧᐣ, » ᐃᑌᐤ.

Cree SRO and English Translation

In the second section of this volume, the stories are given in both the Cree Standard Roman Orthography (SRO) and English translation on facing pages for ease of reference for language learners. This has been standard practice in recent Algonquian text publications (e.g. Ahenakew 1986, 1987b; Bear et al. 1998; Beardy 1988; Ellis 1995, Minde 1997). The conventions of the Cree SRO, as described by Wolfart and Ahenakew (1987), are adhered to with only two minor revisions. Herein, the ***macron*** (or overposed hyphen) is used to indicate vowel length (i.e. ā, ē, ī, ō) in preference to the circumflex (i.e. â, ê, î, ô). Both of these means of marking the long Cree vowels are in common use and, now that macrons are more readily available in computer fonts, we are able to return to and continue the practice of using macrons (cf. Okimāsis 2004; Wolvengrey 2001).

The second modification which will be evident in the presentation of these texts is the special marking used in the Plains and Swampy Cree texts for the "y" and "n" sounds respectively. In Plains Cree, [y] can correspond with either /y/ or /n/ in Swampy Cree and /y/ or /ð/ ("th") in Woods Cree. Similarly, in Swampy Cree, the [n] sound will correspond with either /n/ or /y/ in Plains Cree, and /n/ or /ð/ in Woods Cree, as the examples in Figure 3 illustrate.

Figure 3
Sound Correspondences Across Dialect

	Sounds			
Dialect	**y**	**y/n/ð**		**n**
Plains	pē**y**ak	**ý**ēkaw	ni**ý**a	**n**iýa
Swampy	pē**y**ak	**ń**ēkaw	nī**ń**a	**n**īńa
Woods	pi**y**ak	**th**īkaw	nī**th**a	**n**ītha
translation	"one"	"sand"	"I, me"	"I, me"

Due to these dialect differences, a Plains Cree speaker unfamiliar with the other dialects cannot tell which Plains [y] sounds correspond to common /y/ or to [n] and [ð] in Swampy and Woods respectively. Similarly, a Swampy Cree speaker cannot tell which Swampy [n] sounds correspond to /n/ or to [y] and [ð] sounds in Plains and Woods respectively. Only in Woods Cree are these sounds kept distinct, where common /y/ stays [y], common /n/ stays [n], and the variable

[n]/[y] of Plains/Swampy Cree has a completely different pronunciation, as [ð], similar to the "th" in English "this" or "then" (but not the "th" in "thin"). In order to recognize these differences and make the texts more accessible across the dialects, a special mark has been used with the Plains [y] and Swampy [n] sounds that change across dialect. Changeable Plains [y] is written as an accented "y" (ý), while changeable Swampy [n] is written as an accented "n" (ń). Both of these conventions follow earlier precedents. In editing the Swampy Cree texts in Beardy (1988), Wolfart used the symbol "ñ" for changeable Swampy [n]. In this collection, "ń" is preferred in order to correspond with the usage of "ý" for the Plains Cree texts, used previously but found most extensively to date in Wolvengrey (2001).

Comments particular to each text, whether of its source or its recording and editing, are given on its respective title page. Still, several general comments must be made. Though many of the texts presented here were recorded direct from the spoken word, they have been edited to remove most false starts or speech hesitations and bring them closer in line with the few texts which were pre-scripted and hence did not exhibit such features. On occasion, however, some such hesitations were felt to be integral to the text itself and, especially in the case of the stories told by Elders, attempts were then made to represent the text in a form as close as possible to the spoken original. For this reason, one orthographic convention that can be found in some of the texts is the use of a tilde (~) to represent a break in speech, whether within a word (e.g. *ē-sē-~* ; cf. *ē-sēkōt*) or within a sentence (e.g. *pēyak ~*,). In the latter case, such breaks generally represent pauses with the sentence being revised mid-thought as is normal in actual speech as opposed to the edited written word.

An additional practice that has become quite common in recent Cree text publication is to allow for some representation of "sandhi" or vowel contraction across word boundaries. This allows for a graphic illustration of how the sounds of words can and are blended together in ordinary or rapid speech by fluent speakers. For instance, a word which could be written fully as *ē-at**i**-**a**yāt* is instead rendered as *ē-at-**ā**yāt* with the short vowels [i] and [a] on either side of the hyphen coalescing to a single long [ā] sound. The hyphen is retained, however, to mark the position and occurrence of the vowel contraction. Similarly, across word boundaries, two particles which might be fully spelled out as *ēkos**i** **i**si* are just as likely to be written *ēkos **ī**si*, recognizing the spoken contraction of the two short [i] sounds to a single long [ī], but also leaving a space to mark the word boundary across which the contraction has taken place. Where this has been done within the SRO texts, it has been done without editorial comment. However, such practice is not generally matched in the Syllabics texts where it is much more common to write out the full form of preverbs and other particles.

A final, most-welcome feature of the Cree-English text section is the inclusion of artwork depicting a scene from each story. Late in the production of this volume, a chance conversation concerning the possibility of adding illustrations lead to the fortuitous discovery of the outstanding abilities of 14-year-old Melissa Sanderson. Beginning at the even younger age of four, Melissa has now been creating art for ten years and has already gained recognition and awards for her artistic talents in and around Regina where she currently attends high school. Melissa is a member of the Opāskwēyāk Cree Nation and the daughter of Jeff Sanderson, who edited the eighth text in this collection. Since Jeff's contribution was to edit a text narrated by his own mother, Annabelle, the inclusion of Melissa's artwork means that this volume benefits from the abilities of three generations of the Sanderson family. We are fortunate indeed to be able to conclude each story with Melissa's artwork, and this volume benefits greatly from her contribution.

Cree-English Glossary

The final section of this volume is a Cree-to-English glossary or word list containing all the nouns, verbs, particles, preverbs, etc., found within the Cree texts with accompanying word class and translation. The form of this glossary again closely follows Wolfart and Ahenakew's (1987) lead (cf. also Ahenakew 1986, 1987b; Beardy 1988; Kā-Nīpitēhtēw 1998; Minde 1997, etc.). As such, the glossary includes Cree entries listed in their base or stem form (as indicated with verbs, nouns, preverbs and prenouns by a following hyphen; e.g. *wāpam-* VTA; *pōni-* IPV), and these stems may or may not match the actual spoken form of a full word recognized by a fluent speaker. To a certain extent, then, it is unavoidable with this type of glossary that some knowledge of the structure of Cree words is required to find the parts of words isolated in the entries. However, the current glossary at least has the added feature of including actual textual examples of the full words along with the stem form entries. For example, the word *kā-kī-awāsisīwiyān* is found in text 5, but it is the constituent parts of this word that will be found in the glossary, listed separately under *kā-* IPV, *kī-* IPV, and *awāsisīwi-* VAI. However, all three of these separate references could include as an example of their use, the full word as found in the text (e.g. *kā-kī-awāsisīwiyān* "when I was a child").

Most entries will have examples of this type included.

However, this is not done with particles (IPC), which only occur in isolation in a single form. Similarly, many nouns only occur in their singular forms which are usually the same as the stem forms. Only in cases when a noun occurs in a form other than the singular (e.g. plural, locative, etc.) are textual examples included with the stem entry. For those wishing for more information on stem forms, please consult appropriate grammatical or structural descriptions of Cree such as those found in Ahenakew (1987a), Okimāsis (2004), Wolfart (1973), Wolfart and Ahenakew (1987), and Wolvengrey (2001).

Another feature of this volume's glossary is in the treatment of "dependent" or "bound" noun stems. These are noun stems which cannot occur without some person-marking prefix and they are listed in two places in the glossary. Again, following the glossaries of Ahenakew and Wolfart, all bound stems are given in bare stem form (with preceding hyphen) at the beginning of the glossary. However, since not all readers will be familiar with the analysis of bound stems into their constituent parts minus person indicators, such stems are also listed in the appropriate section of the alphabetized glossary, depending on the form they take in the text. If a bound noun stem is marked with a first person prefix (i.e. /*n-*/, /*ni-*/ or /*nit-*/), it will appear in the bound stem section and the "n" section. For instance, a word like *nitānis*, found in text 8, will be listed twice in the glossary: first in the form of the bound, unmarked stem *-tānis-* and second under the person-marked form *nitānis-*. Similarly, if a bound noun stem is marked with a second person prefix (i.e. /*k-*/, /*ki-*/ or /*kit-*/), it will appear in the bound stem section and the "k" section. If it is marked with one of the third person prefixes, (i.e. /*o-*/, /*ot-*/ or /*w-*/), it will be found in the bound stem section and the "o" or "w" section as appropriate. On rare occasions, a bound stem is cited in the unspecified possessor form (i.e. with prefix /*m-*/ or /*mi-*/) and in such cases, the stem is found in both the bound stem and "m" sections. This double-listing allows easier access to bound stems in the glossary for all readers, regardless of the level of their training in Cree language structure. A similar feature is utilized by Wolvengrey (2001), where all bound stems are given in Vol. 1 (Cree-English) in the appropriate person-marked forms ("m," "n," "o" or "w" sections), but provided as unmarked stem forms in translation of English terms in Vol. 2 (English-Cree).

One final feature of the glossary entries has to do with the multi-dialectal nature of the texts in this volume. Words are listed in the dialect in which they occur in the texts. As explained above, however, the main sound difference between these Cree dialects is marked ("ý" in Plains, "ń" in Swampy, and "th" in Woods) and these markings can be considered as indication of the dialect involved. Words that do not include significant differences across the dialects are listed without comment and can be considered to be the likely form in all three dialects (with some regional variation still possible). In contrast, examples which are clearly from one particular dialect are identified as such with the dialect codes: pC = Plains Cree (or the ý-dialect); sC = Swampy Cree (or the ń-dialect); wC = Woods Cree (or the th-dialect). Often, entries in Woods or Swampy Cree are provided with the Plains Cree form for comparison. It is hoped that all of these features discussed above allow for the stories in this volume to be enjoyed across communities of all the Western Cree dialects.

References

Ahenakew, Freda (ed.). 1986. *kiskinwahamawākan-ācimowinisa / Student Stories*. Algonquian and Iroquoian Linguistics, Memoir 2. Winnipeg: Algonquian and Iroquoian Linguistics.

——. 1987a. *Cree Language Structures: A Cree Approach*. Winnipeg: Pemmican Publications Inc.

—— (ed.). 1987b. *wāskahikaniwiyiniw-ācimowina / Stories of the House People*. Publications of the Algonquian Text Society. Winnipeg: The University of Manitoba Press.

Bear, Glecia, et al. 1998. *kōhkominawak otācimowiniwāwa / Our Grandmothers' Lives as Told in Their Own Words*. Edited and translated by Freda Ahenakew and H.C. Wolfart. Regina: Canadian Plains Research Center.

Beardy, L. 1988. *pisiskiwak kā-pīkiskwēcik / Talking Animals*. Edited by H.C. Wolfart. Algonquian and Iroquoian Linguistics, Memoir 5. Winnipeg: Algonquian and Iroquoian Linguistics.

Ellis, C. Douglas (ed.). 1995. *ātalōhkāna nēsta tipācimowina / Cree Legends and Narratives from the West Coast of James Bay*. Publications of the Algonquian Text Society. Winnipeg: The University of Manitoba Press.

Kā-Nīpitēhtēw, Jim. 1998. *ana kā-pimwēwēhahk okakēskihkēmowina / The Counselling Speeches of Jim Kā-Nīpitēhtēw*. Edited and translated by Freda Ahenakew and H.C. Wolfart. Publications of the Algonquian Text Society. Winnipeg: The University of Manitoba Press.

Minde, Emma. 1997. *kwayask ē-kī-pē-kiskinowāpahtihicik / Their Example Showed Me the Way*. Edited and translated by Freda Ahenakew and H.C. Wolfart. Edmonton: The University of Alberta Press.

Okimāsis, Jean. 2004. *Cree, Language of the Plains*. 2nd, revised edition. Regina: Canadian Plains Research Center.

Wolfart, H.C. 1973. *Plains Cree: A Grammatical Study*. American Philosophical Society Transactions, n.s. 63, pt. 5. Philadelphia.

Wolfart, H.C. and Freda Ahenakew. 1987. "Notes on the Orthography and the Glossary." Pp. 113–25 in Freda Ahenakew (ed.), *wāskahikaniwiyiniw-ācimowina / Stories of the House People*. Winnipeg: The University of Manitoba Press.

Wolvengrey, Arok. 2001. *nēhiýawēwin: itwēwina / Cree: Words*. Volumes 1 & 2. Regina: Canadian Plains Research Center.

ᐊ·ᐃ·ᔭᒑᒋᒍᐃ·ᓂᓯ

(1) ᑖᓂᓯ ᐆᒪ ᐁ ᐃᑌᐧᕽ?

[*Guy Albert, Ahtahkakoop First Nation, SK*]

ᓂᐄᐧ ᐋᒋᒧᐣ ᐆᒪ ᓃᐢᑕ ᐁ ᑮ ᐃᓯ ᐯᐦᑕᒫᐣ ᑲᔮᓴᐢ ᐁ ᑮ ᐋᒋᒧᐟ ᓂᑳᐃᐧᐩ ᐆᑌ ᑭᐢᑕᐱᓈᓂᕽ ᐃᑌ ᑳ ᐄᐧᑭᐟ.

ᐁᓴ ᐊᐊᐧ ᐯᔭᑳᐧᐤ, (ᐊᐊᐧ ᐃᑌᐧᐤ), ᐆᑭ ᓃᓱ ᓅᒋᑫᐧᓯᐊᐧᐠ (ᐃᑌᐧᐤ) ᐆᑌ ᑮᐁᐧᑎᓄᕽ ᓈᓂᑕᐤ, (ᐃᑌᐧᐤ), ᐊᓯ, ᐊᐩ ᐊᐱᐊᐧᐠ ᒦᒋᓱᐃᐧᑲᒥᑯᕽ, (ᐃᑌᐧᐤ), ᐁ ᒪ ᒥᓂᐦᑫᐧᒋᐠ ᐱᐦᑲᐦᑌᐋᐧᐳᐩ ᐁᑲᐧ ᐁ ᒪ ᒦᒋᓱᓯᒋᐠ, (ᐃᑌᐧᐤ). ᐁᑲᐧ ᐁᑯᑕ ᐄᐧᐢᑕ ᓀᑌ ᒪᑌᐧ ᐊᐩ ᐊᐱᐤ ᐊᐊᐧ ᑯᑕᐠ ᓈᐯᐤ, (ᐃᑌᐧᐤ), ᐄᐧᐢᑕ ᐁ ᒪ ᒦᒋᓱᐟ, (ᐃᑌᐧᐤ).

ᑫᑕᐦᑕᐁᐧ ᐁᓴ ᐁ ᒪᑌᐧ ᑌᐹᐧᑖᐟ ᐅᔫᑭᓂᑫᐊᐧ, ᐅᒥᓯ ᐁᓴ ᑳ ᐃᑖᐟ: « *Hey waitress, could you please bring me some yam?* » ᒪᑌᐧ ᐃᑌᐧᐤ ᐁᓴ.

ᒥᑐᓂ ᐁᓴ ᑳ ᒥᓯ ᐹᐦᐱᐸᔨᐟ ᐊᐊᐧ ᐯᔭᐠ ᓅᒋᑫᐧᓯᐤ ᐁ ᑑᐢᑭᓈᐟ ᐁ ᐄᐧᐦᑕᒪᐋᐧᐟ ᐄᐧᒉᐋᐧᑲᓇ, « ᐄᐦᐄ, ᓂᒫᐦᑯᐢ, ᑭᐯᐦᑕᐋᐧᐤ ᒌ ᐊᓇ ᓈᐯᐤ? » ᐃᑌᐧᐤ. « ᓇᒨᔭ ᐊᓇ ᐊᐦᔮ ᐁ ᑲᐢᑭᐦᑖᐟ ᑫᐧᔭᐢᐠ *cham* ᑲ ᐃᑌᐧᐟ, » ᐁᓴ ᐃᑌᐤ.

ᐁᑯᓯ ᐆᒪ ᐁᑯᑕ ᐁ ᑭᐱᐦᑎᐠ ᐆᒪ ᓂᑖᒋᒧᐣ.

(2) ᑮᒁᕀ ᐊᓇ ᑮᑿᕀ?

[Doreen Martell, Waterhen First Nation, SK]

ᐯᔭᒁᐤ ᐁᓴ ᐊᐘ ᓀᐦᐃᔭᐤ ᓈᓯᐍᐤ ᐃᐢᐲ ᓂᐢᑕᒼ ᒨᓂᔮᐘᐠ ᑮ ᑕᑯᐦᑌᒋᐠ. ᓂᑕᐏ ᐲᐦᑐᑵᐤ ᐁᓴ ᓃᒥᐦᐃᑐᐏᑲᒥᑯᕽ.

ᑫᑕᐦᑕᐌ ᑳ ᐅᑎᓈᐟ ᐊᐘ ᐯᔭᐠ ᓈᐯᐤ ᑮᑿᔭ, ᒣᑐᓂ ᐁᑿ ᐁᑯᑕ ᐹᐦ ᐲᒥᐦᑕᐘᑫᓀᐤ, ᐁ ᒫᐦ ᒨᐢᑯᐱᑖᐟ, « ᑌᐣ, ᑌᐣ, ᑌᐣ, ᐄᐠ! ᑌᐣ, ᑌᐣ, ᑌᐣ, ᐄᐠ! »

ᐁᑯᓯ ᐁᓴ ᐁ ᔮᓂ ᐲᒥᐦᑕᐘᑫᓈᐟ ᑳ ᐅᑎᓇᕽ ᐁᓴ ᒥᐢᒋᑯᐢ ᐁ ᒥᓯ ᓅᒋᐦᐋᐟ. ᐊᔨᐚᐠ ᒥᓯ ᒫᑐᔭᐘ ᐆᐦᐃ ᑮᑿᔭ. ᑳ ᐸᓯᑰᐸᐦᑖᒋᐠ ᐁᓴ ᐆᑭ ᒨᓂᔮᐘᐠ ᐁ ᒫᒋ ᓅᑎᓂᑐᒋᐠ.

« ᓃᐢᑕ ᐊᐘ ᐯᔭᐠ ᓅᒋᑵᓯᐤ ᓂᐯ ᐅᑎᐦᑎᓂᐠ, ᒣᑐᓂ ᓂᒥᓯ ᐸᑲᒪᐦᐚᐤ ᐁᑯᓯ ᓂᑕᐸᓰᐣ. »

(3) ᑮᑲᐧᐩ ᐊᓇ?
[Neil Sapp, Little Pine First Nation, SK]

ᑲᔮᐢ ᐆᒪ ᐁ ᑮ ᐃᐢᐸᔨᐠ.

ᐁᔭᑳᐧᐤ ᐁᓴ ᐆᑭ ᓀᐦᐃᔭᐤ ᒫᒦᐃᐧᔨᓂᐊᐧᐠ ᑳ ᑳᐦᒋᑎᓈᒋᐠ ᐱᓯᐢᑭᐊᐧ. ᒫᑲ ᒨᐩ ᑮ ᓂᓯᑕᐃᐧᓇᐁᐧᐊᐧᐠ ᑮᑳᐧᔭ ᐊᐊᐧ. ᒥᑐᓂ ᑳᐦ ᑭᑖᐸᒣᐊᐧᐠ. « ᑖᓂᓯ ᒫᑲ ᑲ ᑑᑕᐋᐧᓇᐤ? »

« ᑲ ᑮᐁᐧᐦᑕᐦᐚᐧᓇᐤ, » ᐃᑌᐧᐤ ᐊᐊᐧ ᐯᔭᐠ. « ᑲ ᓂᑕᐤ ᐚᐧᐸᐦᑎᐦᐚᐧᓇᐤ ᒪᐢᑭᐦᑮᐃᐧᔨᓂᐤ. ᑲᐦᑭᔭᐤ ᑮᑲᐧᐩ ᒪᐢᑭᐦᑮᐃᐧᔨᓂᐤ ᑭᐢᑫᔨᐦᑕᑦ, ᐊᐦᐴ ᐁ ᓈᑕᐃᐧᐦᐃᐁᐧᐟ ᒦᓇ. »

« ᐊᐦᐚᐤ. » ᐁᑯᓯ ᐃᑐᐦᑕᐦᐁᐊᐧᐠ.

ᒣᑐᓂ ᑳᐦ ᑭᑖᐸᒣᐤ ᐊᐊᐧ ᒪᐢᑭᐦᑮᐃᐧᔨᓂᐤ. « ᒫᐧᐨ, » ᐃᑌᐧᐤ. « ᓇᒨᔭ ᐄᐧᐦᑳᐨ ᐁᑯᑐᐊᐧ ᓂᐯ ᓇᑭᐢᑲᐚᐧᐤ, » ᐃᑌᐧᐤ. « ᓇᒨᐩ ᐄᐧᐦᑳᐨ ᐁᑯᑐᐊᐧ ᓂᑑᐦ ᐚᐧᐸᒫᐤ, » ᐁᑌᐧᐤ. « ᒥᐢᑕᐦᐃ ᑮᑲᐧᐩ ᓂᑭᐢᑫᔨᐦᑌᐣ ᒫᑲ, ᒫᑲ ᓇᒨᔭ ᑮᑲᐧᐩ ᐁᑯᑐᐊᐧ. ᐚᐦᐊ, ᒫᑲ ᓇᐊᐧᐨ ᐅᐱᒥᐸᔨᐦᒋᑫᐤ, ᑲᐦᑭᔭᐤ ᑮᑲᐧᐩ ᐃᐧᔭ ᑭᐢᑫᔨᐦᑕᑦ, ᐃᑐᐦᑕᐦᐃᕽ ᐅᑭᒫᐦᑳᐣ ᐄᐧᑭᐚᐧᕽ. »

ᐁᑯᓯ ᐃᑐᐦᑕᐦᐁᐊᐧᐠ ᐆᐦᐃ ᐅᑭᒫᐦᑳᐣ ᐄᐧᑭᐚᐧᕽ. ᐚᐧᐸᐦᑎᐦᐁᐊᐧᐠ. « ᑭᑭᐢᑫᔨᒫᐤ ᒌ ᐊᐊᐧ ᑮᑲᐧᐩ ᐊᔭ? » ᑯᓂᑕ ᐁ ᐃᑌᐧᒋᐠ.

ᑭᑖᐸᒣᐤ. « ᒪᐦᑎ ᐯᓯᐤ, » ᐃᑌᐧᐤ ᐊᐊᐧ ᐅᑭᒫᐦᑳᐣ. « ᐚᐦᐊ, » ᐃᑌᐧᐤ. « ᒣᑐᓂ ᐊᐱᓰᓯᓯᐤ ᐁᑲᐧ ᒣᑐᓂ ᓈᐯᓯᐢ ᐁ ᐃᓯᓈᑯᓯᐟ. ᐁᑲᐧ ᒣᑐᓂ ᐊᔭ ᐁ ᑭᓈᐧᐯᑲᓂᔨᐠ ᒥᓲᐩ ᐁ ᐊᔮᐟ ᐃᔨᓂᑐ ᒧᐢᑐᓴᐠ, » ᑯᓂᑕ ᐁ ᐃᑌᐧᐟ.

« ᐁᑲᐧ ᓃᓱ ᒥᓯᑕ ᐁ ᐊᔮᐟ ᐁᑲᐧ ᓃᓱ ᒥᒋᐦᒋᔭ, » ᐃᑌᐧᐤ. « ᐁᑲᐧ ᐁ ᒦᐦᔭᐁᐧᑲᓵᑫᓯᐟ, » ᐃᑌᐧᐤ. « *A Cowboy* ᐊᐊᐧ ᑳ ᒥᐢᑲᐚᓴᐠ, » ᑯᓂᑕ ᐁ ᐃᑌᐧᐟ.

(4) ᐁ ᓰᐯᑭᐢᑎᑳᐧᓀᓂᓱᐟ
*[Bealiqué Kahmahkotayo,
Little Pine First Nation, SK]*

ᐯᔭᑳᐧᐤ ᐁᓴ ᒨᔭ ᑲᔮᐢ ᐆᒪ ᓂᑳᐃᐧᐩ ᐊᐧ *Mary Jane* ᑳ ᑮ ᐃᑎᑯᐟ ᓄᐦᑖᐃᐧᔭ *Horace*ᐊᐧ ᑲ ᓰᐯᑭᐢᑎᑳᐧᓀᓈᐟ. ᑖᐱᐢᑰᐨ ᐁᓴ ᐊᐧ ᓄᐦᑖᐃᐧᐩ ᐁ ᑮ ᑯᐢᑕᕽ ᓂᐱᐩ, ᐁ ᑮ ᐊᐩ ᐃᑌᔨᐦᑕᒫᐣ ᒫᓇ. ᐁᑯᓯ ᐁᓴ ᓄᐦᑖᐃᐧᐩ ᑮ ᓂᑕᐃᐧ ᓰᐯᑭᐢᑎᑳᐧᓀᓂᓱᐤ ᐁᑯᐢᐲᕽ ᐁᑲᐧ. ᑭᓀᐧᓲᐢ ᐁᓴ ᐆᒪ ᐁᑲᐧ ᐁ ᓅᒋᐦᑖᐟ ᑕ ᓰᐯᑭᐢᑎᑳᐧᓀᓂᓱᐟ ᐊᐧ ᓄᐦᑖᐃᐧᐩ. « ᑖᓂᓯ ᐁᑎᑫᐧ ᐁ ᐃᑕᐦᑲᒥᑭᓯᐟ? » ᑮ ᐊᐩ ᐃᑌᔨᐦᑕᒼ ᐁᑲᐧ ᐊᐧ ᓂᑳᐃᐧᐩ. ᐁᑯᓯ ᐁᓴ ᑳ ᓂᑕᐋᐧᐯᓇᐋᐧᐟ ᐆᐦᐃ ᓄᐦᑖᐃᐧᔭ. ᓂᑳᐃᐧᐩ ᐁᓴ ᐁᑲᐧ ᑳ ᓂᑕᐃᐧ ᒪᑌᐧᐦᑕᐦᐃᑫᐟ ᐁᑯᑕ ᐃᐢᑳᐧᐦᑌᒥᕽ. ᑮ ᑮᓯ ᓰᐯᑭᐢᑎᑳᐧᓀᐤ ᐁᓴ ᐊᐧ ᓄᐦᑖᐃᐧᐩ ᐋᓴᐩ. ᑳ ᐸᓱᐟ ᐁᓴ ᓂᑳᐃᐧᐩ ᐆᒪ ᑮᑲᐧᐩ ᐯᔭᑳᐧᐣ ᐁ ᐃᓯᒫᑲᐧᕽ ᑳ ᓰᐯᑳᐱᑌᕽ ᒫᓇ. ᓄᐦᑖᐃᐧᐩ ᐁᓴ ᐊᐧ ᐋᓴᐩ ᐁ ᑮᓯ ᑳᓰᐦᑫᐧᐟ ᐁᑲᐧ ᐁ ᐊᐧᐁᐧᓰᐟ. ᑖᓂᑌ ᐁᑎᑫᐧ ᑳ ᑮ ᐄᐧ ᐃᑐᐦᑌᒋᐠ ᐆᑭ ᓂᓃᑭᐦᐃᑯᒫᐊᐧᐠ ᑳ ᑮᓯᑳᐠ ᐁᑯᐢᐲᕽ.

ᐁᑯᐢᐲᕽ ᐁᓴ ᓃᑎᓵᓇᐠ ᐁ ᑮ ᑭᔮᑲᐊᐧᑭᐠ. ᐁ ᐸ ᐹᐦᐱᔮᕽ ᐁᓴ ᐁᑲᐧ ᐁ ᐋᒋᒧᐢᑖᑐᔮᕽ, ᐁ ᐃᑖᒋᒨᔮᕽ ᑮᑲᐧᔭ ᑳ ᑮ ᐃᓯ ᐃᑑᑕᒫᕽ ᑲᔮᐢ ᐊᐢᐱᐣ ᑳ ᑮ ᐋᐧᐸᒥᑐᔮᕽ. ᓂᒪᐋᐧᓯᒥᓯᓈᓇᐠ ᒦᓇ ᓂᑮ ᐋᒋᒫᓈᓇᐠ ᑖᓂᓯ ᑳ ᑮ ᐯ ᐊᐩ ᐃᑕᐦᑲᒥᑭᓯᒋᐠ.

ᐁᑯᓯ ᐁᓴ ᐊᐧ ᓄᐦᑖᐃᐧᐩ ᑳ ᐯ ᓵᑫᐁᐧᐟ ᐃᑌ ᐁᑯᑕ ᑳ ᐊᐩ ᐊᐱᔩᕽ. ᑫᑕᐦᑕᐁᐧ ᐁᓴ ᑳ ᐸᓱᔮᕽ ᑮᑲᐧᐩ ᑖᐱᐢᑰᐨ ᑳ ᓰᐯᑳᐱᑌᒫᑲᐧᕽ. ᐁᑯᓯ ᐁᓴ ᐁᑲᐧ ᓂᑳᐃᐧᐩ ᐊᐧ ᑳ ᐅᑎᓇᕽ ᐊᓂᒪ ᐹᐦᑯᐦᑫᐧᐦᐅᐣ ᓄᐦᑖᐃᐧᔭ ᐅᐁᐧᐢᒪᑳᔨᐊᐧ ᐁ ᐄᐧ ᐹᓴᕽ, ᑳ ᓲᐦᑫᒫᑲᐧᕽ ᐁᓴ ᑮᑲᐧᐩ ᑖᐱᐢᑰᐨ ᐁ ᑮᓯ ᓰᐯᑳᐱᑌᐦᐅᔨᐟ ᓄᐦᑖᐃᐧᔭ ᒫᑲ ᐁᓴ ᐅᐁᐧᐢᒪᑳᔨᐊᐧ

ᐊᓂᑕ ᐁ ᒥᔮᐦᑕᕽ ᐊᐊᐧ ᓂᑳᐃᐧᐩ. ᑳ ᑲᑫᐧᒥᒫᐟ ᐁᓴ
ᓅᐦᑖᐃᐧᔭ ᑮᑳᐧᔭ ᐁ ᐋᐸᒋᐦᑖᔨᐟ ᑲ ᐅᐦᒋ ᓰᐯᑭᐢᑎᑳᐧᒍᓂᓱᔨᐟ.
ᓅᐦᑖᐃᐧᐩ ᐁᓴ ᑳ ᐃᑖᐟ ᐆᐦᐃ ᓂᑳᐃᐧᔭ ᐁᓴ ᐋᓴᐩ ᐆᒪ
ᐁ ᑮᓯ ᓵᐳᐸᑖᐟ ᐅᐁᐧᐢᒪᑳᓴ, ᐁᑯᓯ ᐁᓴ ᐱᑯ ᑮᑲᐧᐩ
ᑳ ᐃᑌᔨᐦᑕᕽ ᓅᐦᑖᐃᐧᐩ ᐊᐊᐧ ᑳ ᓵᒥᓇᕽ ᑳ ᒨᓯᐦᑖᐠ ᐁᓴ
ᑮᑲᐧᐩ ᑖᐱᐢᑰᐨ ᓰᐯᑭᐢᑎᑳᐧᒍ ᓰᐯᑭᓂᑲᐣ. ᐁᐊᐧᑯ ᐁᓴ ᐱᑯ
ᑳ ᒥᐢᑲᕽ. ᐁᑯᓯ ᐁᓴ ᑳ ᒥᓯ ᑭᐢᐸᑲᐧᐢᑖᐟ ᐁᑲᐧ ᐅᐁᐧᐢᒪᑳᓯᕽ.
ᐊᐧᐦᐋᐧ, ᓂᑳᐃᐧᐩ ᐁᓴ ᑳ ᑭᓯᐋᐧᓯᐟ, ᑫᑳᐨ ᓅᐦᑖᐃᐧᔭ
ᐁ ᐸᑲᒪᐦᐋᐧᐟ. « ᐁᑯᓯ ᒫᓇ ᐆᒪ ᐁᑯᓰᓯ
ᐁ ᓂᐦᑖ ᐹᐦᐱᐦᐃᑲᐃᐧᔮᐣ, ᐁᑯᓰᓯ ᐁ ᓂᑕᐁᐧᔨᐦᑕᒪᐣ
ᓇᓭᐢᑕᐤ, » ᑳ ᐃᑖᐟ ᐁᓴ ᐊᐊᐧ ᓅᐦᑖᐃᐧᔭ. ᓅᐦᑖᐃᐧᐩ
ᐁᓴ ᐊᓂᒪ ᓯᐯᑳᐱᑌᐃᐧ ᐸᓴᑲᐧᐦᐃᑲᐣ ᐁᓴ ᐊᓂᒪ
ᑳ ᐋᐸᒋᐦᑖᐟ.

ᐁᑯᓯ ᐁᓴ ᓅᐦᑖᐃᐧᐩ ᑳ ᐹᐦᐱᐟ, « ᐁᐣᐨ, ᐋᐧᒋᐢᑕᑳᐨ,
ᐁ ᐃᑌᔨᐦᑕᒫᐣ ᐁᑎᑫᐧ ᐊᓂᒪ ᓰᐯᑭᐢᑎᑳᐧᒍᐃᐧ ᓰᐯᑭᓂᑲᐣ. »
ᑲᐦᑭᔭᐤ ᓂᐹᐦᐱᓈᐣ ᐁᑲᐧ. ᐁᑯᓯ ᐁᑲᐧ ᓂᑳᐃᐧᐩ
ᑳ ᐲᐦᑐᑫᐧᔭᐦᑮᓈᐟ ᓅᐦᑖᐃᐧᔭ ᐁ ᓂᑕᐃᐧ ᓰᐯᑭᐢᑎᑳᐧᒍᓈᐟ
ᑲᐧᔭᐢᐠ. ᓂᐢᑖᐧᐤ ᐁᓴ ᐊᐊᐧ ᓂᑳᐃᐧᐩ ᑳ ᓰᐯᑭᐢᑎᑳᐧᒍᓈᐟ
ᐊᓂᐦᐃ ᓅᐦᑖᐃᐧᔭ ᐅᓵᒼ ᐁ ᓰᐦᑫᒫᑲᐧᓂᔨᐠ ᓰᐯᑳᐱᑌᐃᐧ
ᐸᓴᑲᐧᐦᐃᑲᐣ ᐅᐁᐧᐢᒪᑳᓯᔨᕽ. ᐁᑯᓯ ᐁᓴ ᓂᑳᐃᐧᐩ
ᑳ ᓇᐦᐊᐢᑖᐟ ᐊᓂᒪ ᓰᐯᑳᐱᑌᐃᐧ ᐸᓴᑲᐧᐦᐃᑲᐣ ᐁᑲᐧ ᒦᓇ
ᐁ ᐅᓵᐸᒫᐟ ᒫᓇ ᐆᐦᐃ ᓅᐦᑖᐃᐧᔭ ᑳ ᐄᐧ ᓰᐯᑭᐢᑎᑳᐧᒍᔨᐟ.

ᐋᐧᐦᐊᐩ. ᒣᑐᓂ, ᓇᒨᔭ ᐁᐊᐧᑯ ᐄᐧᐦᑳᐨ ᓂᐊᐧᓂᑭᐢᑭᓯᓈᐣ
ᑫᑳᐨ ᐁ ᓂᐸᐦᐃ ᐹᐦᐱᔮᕽ ᑲᐦᑭᔭᐤ ᐁ ᐊᐧᐃᐧᔭᑌᔨᐦᑕᒪᐋᐧᔮᐦᑭᐠ
ᓅᐦᑖᐄᐧᓈᐣ ᐁᑲᐧ ᓂᑳᐄᐧᓈᐣ ᐁ ᑫᐦᑌ ᐊᔨᐃᐧᒋᐠ ᐁᑲᐧ ᑫᔮᐱᐨ
ᐁ ᓵᑭᐦᐃᑐᒋᐠ. ᒣᑐᓂ ᒥᐢᑕᐦᐃ ᐁᑯᐢᐲᕽ ᑕᐦᑐ ᑮᓯᑳᐤ
ᓂᑮ ᐹᐦᐱᓈᐣ ᑲᐦᑭᔭᐤ ᐁᑯᑕ ᑳ ᑭᔪᑳᑐᔮᕽ. ᐊᐋᐧᓯᓴᐠ
ᐄᐧᐢᑕᐋᐧᐤ ᑮ ᐹᐦᐱᐊᐧᐠ, ᐋᑎᐦᐟ ᒨᔭ ᑮ ᑭᐢᑫᔨᐦᑕᒪᐧᐠ
ᓀᐦᐃᔭᐃᐧᑐᑕᒧᐃᐧᐣ.

ᑫᔮᐱᐨ ᒫᓇ ᐆᒪ ᐋᒋᒧᐃᐧᐣ ᓂᑖᑐᑌᓈᐣ ᐃᐢᐲᕽ ᓄᐦᑖᐄᐧᓈᐣ ᑳ ᑮ ᑲᑫᐧ ᓲᐯᑭᐢᑎᑳᐧᑐᓂᓯᐟ. ᐁᐊᐧᑯ ᒫᓇ ᐆᒪ ᒥᔪ ᐋᒋᒧᐃᐧᐣ ᓂᑭᐢᑭᓯᓈᐣ ᑳ ᐄᐧ ᒫᒋ ᑭᓯᐋᐧᓯᔮᕽ ᐆᑭ ᓃᑎᓵᓇᐠ.

ᐁᑯᓯ.

(5) ᒎᖬ ᓀᖬ *Indian*
*[Solomon Ratt, Stanley Mission, SK]**

ᑲᔮᐢ ᒫᓇ ᑳ ᑫ ᐊᐋᐧᓯᓭᐃᐧᔮᐣ ᐆᑌ ᒫᓇ ᓂᑫ ᓂᑕᐃᐧ ᐊᔭᒥᐦᒥᑳᓈᐣ ᑭᐢᑕᐱᓈᓂᕽ ᐃᑯᑌ ᒫᓇ ᐁ ᓂᑕᐃᐧ ᑭᐢᑭᓇᐧᐦᐊᒫᑯᓯᔮᕽ. ᑕᐦᑐ ᐊᐢᑭᐩ ᒫᓇ ᑕᑳᐧᑭ ᐯᓯᑦ ᑳ ᑫ ᒫᒥᐦᑖᔮᕽ ᐁ ᑫ ᓂᑕᐃᐧ ᑳᐦ ᑭᐢᑭᓇᐧᐦᐊᒫᑯᓯᔮᕽ ᐃᑯᑕ ᐆᒪ *residential schools* ᑳ ᑫ ᐃᒥᑳᑌᑭ, ᐃᑯᑌ ᑳ ᑫ ᐃᑐᐦᑌᔮᐣ, ᐋᐦ, *Prince Albert Indian Student Residences* ᑫ ᐃᓯᖬᐦᑳᑌᐤ ᐃᔭᑯ ᐊᓂᒪ. ᐁᑲᐧ ᐁᑯᑕ ᒫᓇ ᒥᐢᑕᐦᐃ ᒫᓇ ᐊᐋᐧᓯᓭᐠ ᑫ ᑭᑎᒫᑭᓯᐊᐧᐠ ᒥᐢᑕᐦᐃ ᒫᓇ ᑫ ᒫᐦ ᒪᐁᐧᐦᑳᑌᐊᐧᐠ ᐅᓀᑭᐦᐃᑯᐋᐧᐊᐧ.

ᐊᔭ, ᒉᓇ ᒥᐢᑕᐦᐃ ᒉᓇ ᒫᓇ ᓂᑫ ᒎᒥᑭᐦᑖᓈᐣ ᒫᓇ ᑕᐦᑖᐧᐤ ᑳ ᒫᑎᓇᐃᐧ ᑫᓯᑳᐠ, ᐁᑯᐢᐯ ᒫᓇ ᓂᑫ ᑲᓇᐋᐧᐸᐦᑌᓈᐣ, ᐋᐦ, ᒋᑳᐢᑌᐸᖬᐦᒋᑲᓇ, *picture shows* ᓂᑫ ᐃᓯᖬᐦᑳᑌᓈᐣ ᒫᓇ. ᐃᔭᑯᓂ ᒫᓇ, ᒥᑐᓂ ᒫᓇ ᓂᑫ ᒫᐦ ᒎᒥᑭᐦᑖᓈᐣ ᑳ ᐴᓂ ᐋᐧᐸᐦᑕᒫᕽ ᐁᐧᖬ ᐊᖬᐢᐠ ᒫᓇ ᐁ ᓂᑕᐃᐧ ᒉᑕᐁᐧᔮᕽ ᐊᐧᖬᐁᐧᑎᒥᕽ ᑖᐱᐢᑰᐨ ᒫᓇ ᓀᖬᓈᐣ, ᐋᐦ, *Pirates* ᒫᓇ ᓂᑫ ᒉᑕᐋᐧᓈᐣ ᐃᑲᐧ ᒉᓇ *Cowboys and Indians.* ᐃᑯᓯ ᒫᓇ ᑳ ᑫ ᐃᓯ ᒉᑕᐁᐧᔮᕽ, ᐃᑲᐧ ᐆᒪ ᑳ ᑫ ᐯ ᐃᓯ ᐅᐦᐱᑮᔮᕽ ᐆᒪ ᒥᑐᓂ ᒫᓇ, ᐋᐦ ..., ᓂᑫ ᐁᐧᓀᖬᒥᓱᓈᐣ, ᒎᖬ ᓀᖬᓈᐣ ᓀᐦᐃᖬᐊᐧᐠ ᑕ ᑫ ᐃᓯ ᐱᒫᑎᓯᔮᕽ ᐁ ᐃᑎᑲᐃᐧᔮᕽ ᒫᓇ. ᐃᑯᓯ ᒫᓇ ᑳ ᑫ ᐃᓯ ᐅᐦᐱᑭᐦᐃᑲᐃᐧᔮᕽ ᐁᑯᑕ ᑭᐢᑭᓇᐧᐦᐊᒫᑐᐃᐧᑲᒥᑯᕽ.

ᒫᑲ ᐱᔭᑳᐧᐤ ᐆᒪ ᐁ ᑫ ᓂᑕᐃᐧ ᑲᓇᐋᐧᐸᐦᑕᒫᕽ *Cowboys and Indians* ᒋᑳᐢᑌᐸᖬᐦᒋᑲᐣ, *John Wayne* ᐃᑯᑕ ᒉᓇ

* This text is presented in Woods Cree Syllabics (e.g. ᐁ = ī, etc.); see Introduction.

ᑳ ᑫ ᐊᔮᐟ, ᐁ ᑫ ᓅᑯᓯᐟ, ᓂᑫ ᒣᐦᑭᓀᐣ, ᐃᔭᑯ ᐊᓂᒪ ᓂᑫ ᒣᐦᑳᐸᐦᑌᐣ, ᓂᒥᖧᐧᖨᐦᑌᐣ ᑕ ᐚᐸᐦᑕᒫᐣ, *John Wayne* ᑕ ᑲᓇᐚᐸᒪᐠ. ᐃᑲᐧ ᒫᓇ ᑳ ᑫ ᐴᓂ ᐚᐸᐦᑕᒫᕽ ᐃᔭᑯᓂ ᐊᔭ ᒫᓇ ᓂᑫ ᓂᑕᐃᐧ ᒣᑕᐚᓈᐣ *Cowboys and Indians* ᒫᑲ ᒫᓇ ᐁ ᑫ ᒫᐊᐧᓴᑯᓂᑐᔮᕽ. ᐋᐦ, ᐱᔭᑳᐧᔪᕽ ᐃᑕ *Indians* ᐁᑲᐧ ᐱᔭᑳᐧᔪᕽ ᑯᑕᐠ *Cowboys;* ᐃᑲᐧ ᒫᓇ ᓀᖬ ᑲᐯ ᒫᓇ ᓀᖬ ᐃᐢᑫᐧᔮᓂᕽ ᑳ ᑫ ᐅᑎᓂᑲᐃᐧᔮᐣ. ᐃᑲᐧ ᑫᑕᐦᑕᐁᐧ ᐆᒪ ᐆᑕ ᐱᔭᐠ ᑫᓯᑳᐤ ᓂᑫ ᐊᑎ ᐅᑎᓂᑲᐃᐧᐣ, *Indians* ᐁᓴ ᓀᖬ ᑕ ᐊᔮᔮᐣ. ᐋᐦ, ᓇᒨᖬ ᓂᑫ ᒣᐦᑫᖨᐦᑌᐣ, ᓇᒨᖬ ᓀᖬ *Indian* ᓂᑫ ᓅᐦᑌ ᐃᑕᑭᓱᐣ ᐃᑯᑕ.

« ᒨᖬ ᓀᖬ *Indian,* » ᓂᑫ ᐃᑖᐧᐣ. « ᓇᒨᖬ ᓂᐁᐧ *India*ᓂᐃᐧᐣ! » ᐁ ᐃᑌᐧᔮᐣ.

« ᐁᐩ, » ᐃᑌᐧᐤ ᐆᑕ ᐱᔭᐠ ᓈᐯᐤ ᑳ ᑫ ᑲᓇᐁᐧᖨᒥᑯᔮᕽ, *supervisor* ᑳ ᑫ ᐃᑎᐦᐟ; « ᐁᐩ, ᑖᐯᐧ ᑭᑭᑎᒫᑭᓯᐣ ᐃᑯᓯ ᐁ ᐃᑌᖨᐦᑕᒪᐣ. *Indian* ᐊᖨᐢᐠ ᐆᒪ ᑫᖬ ᑕ ᑫ ᐃᑌᖨᒥᓱᔭᐣ ᐃᑯᓯ ᐃᓯ ᐁ ᐃᑕᑭᓱᔭᐣ, » ᓂᑫ ᐃᑎᑲᐃᐧᐣ.

ᐃᑯᓯ.

(6) ᐁ ᑖᐦ ᑖᐸᑫᐧᕽ
[*Gilbert Starr, Starblanket First Nation, SK*]

ᓂᑲ ᐋᒋᒧᐣ ᓅᐦᑖᐃᐧᕀ ᐁᑲᐧ ᓅᐦᒫᐃᐧᐢ ᐁ ᑮ ᐋᒋᒧᒋᐠ ᒣᑳᐧᐨ ᐁ ᐱᒫᑎᓯᒋᐠ ᐆᑕ. ᑮ ᐸᐹ ᑭᔦᑳᑐᐊᐧᐠ ᐊᔨᐢᐠ ᑲᔮᐢ ᑭᓭᔨᓂᐊᐧᐠ ᐆᑕ ᐃᐢᑯᓂᑲᓂᕽ. ᑌᐸᑯᐦᑊ ᐃᐦᑕᓯᐊᐧᐠ ᓅᐦᒫᐃᐧᓴᐠ ᑭᑭ ᓅᐦᑖᐃᐧᕀ.

ᑕᐦᑐ ᑎᐸᐢᑳᐤ ᐊᓂᒪ ᑮ ᐯ ᐃᑐᐦᑌᐊᐧᐠ ᐁ ᐯ ᓂᑕᐋᐧᐸᐦᑐᒋᐠ ᑖᓂᓯ ᐁ ᑮ ᐃᓯ ᐊᑐᐢᑫᒋᐠ ᑕᐦᑐ ᑮᓯᑳᐤ ᐁᑲᐧ ᐁ ᐱᒫᒋᐦᐋᐧᐊᐧᓱᒋᐠ ᐄᐧᐢᑕᐋᐧᐤ. ᑮ ᑖᐸᑫᐧᐊᐧᐠ ᐋᐧᐳᓴᐧ ᑕᐦᑐ ᑮᓯᑳᐤ, ᑮ ᓈᑕᑫᐧᐊᐧᐠ ᐁ ᐅᐦᒋ ᐊᓴᒫᐊᐧᓱᒋᐠ ᐄᐧᐢᑕᐋᐧᐤ. ᓇᒪ ᑮᑲᐧᕀ ᑮ ᐅᐦᒋ ᐄᐧᒋᐦᐋᐧᐊᐧᐠ, ᓇᒎᓴ ᑖᐱᐢᑰᐨ ᐆᒪ ᐊᓄᐦᐨ ᐊᔨᓯᔨᓂᐊᐧᐠ ᐁ ᑭᐦᒋ ᐄᐧᒋᐦᐃᐦᒋᐠ. ᐃᐧᔭᐋᐧᐤ ᐱᑯ ᐁ ᑲᑫᐧ ᐃᓯ ᐱᒫᒋᐦᐅᒋᐠ ᐁ ᐃᓯ ᐱᐦᑯᐦᑖᒋᐠ ᑮᑲᐧᕀ ᑲ ᒦᒋᒋᐠ ᐁᐊᐧᑯᓂ, ᐁᐊᐧᑯ ᐱᑯ ᐋᑕᐃᐧᔭ ᑮ ᐊᓴᒫᐊᐧᐠ ᓈᓂᔮᐤ ᐅᑭᒫᓈᕽ ᐅᐦᒋ. ᐋᐦ, ᑕᐦᑐ ᐋᐧᐸᐣ ᑮ ᓈᑕᑫᐧᐊᐧᐠ, ᐋᐧᐳᓴᐧ ᐁ ᑲᑫᐧ ᓂᐸᐦᐋᐧᒋᐠ ᐁᑲᐧ ᓅᐦᑖᐃᐧᕀ ᑮ ᑳᐦ ᑭᒧᑕᒫᐠ ᐁᓴ, ᐋ, ᓯᐦᑯᓴ ᐆᐦᐃ, ᐁ ᑮ ᒧᐋᐧᔨᐟ ᒫᓇ ᐅᐋᐧᐳᓱᒪ.

ᐋ, ᑫᑕᐦᑕᐁᐧ ᐁᓴ, «« *ᓂᑖᐸᑲᐧᒪᐋᐧᐤ ᐊᓄᐦᐨ ᐊᐊᐧ ᑳ ᑳᐦ ᑭᒧᑕᒪᐃᐧᐟ ᓯᐦᑯᐢ*, » ᓂᑕᕀ ᐃᑖᐧᐣ, » ᐃᑌᐧᐤ. ᐁᑯᓯ. ᒫᐸᑳᐧᓂᐢ ᐁᑲᐧ ᐅᓰᐦᑖᐤ, ᐊᐱᓰᓯᓯᐊᐧᐠ ᐊᔨᐢᐠ ᐆᑭ ᓯᐦᑯᓴᐠ ᐅᐢᒋᑲᐧᓂᐢ ᑲ ᒥᔦ ᑌᐱᐦᑎᓂᔨᐠ ᐁᐊᐧᑯᔨᑯᕽ ᐊᕀ ᐃᓰᐦᑖᐤ ᐊᓂᒪ ᒫᐸᑳᐧᓂᐢ. ᐁᑯᓯ.

ᑕᑯᐦᑌᐤ ᐁ ᐅᑖᑯᓯᓂᔨᐠ ᑳ ᐄᐧᐦᑕᒪᐋᐧᐟ ᐁᑲᐧ ᓂᑳᐃᐧᔭ, « ᐦᐋᐧᐤ, ᓅᑐᑫᓯᐤ. ᓂᑳᐦ ᑭᒧᑕᒫᐠ ᓯᐦᑯᐢ ᑫ ᐋᐧᐸᕽ ᓂᑲ ᑖᐸᑳᐧᑖᐤ ᓂᑮ ᐅᓰᐦᑕᒪᐋᐧᐤ ᒫᐸᑳᐧᓂᐢ, » ᐃᑌᐤ ᓂᑳᐃᐧᔭ. ᐁᑯᓯ, ᓇᒎᓴ ᓈᓂᑕᐤ ᐊᕀ ᐃᑌᐧᐤ ᓂᑳᐃᐧᕀ. ᐁᑯᓯ ᑲᐃᐧᔨᒧᐊᐧᐠ ᐋᓴᕀ, ᐋᓴᕀ ᐁᓴ ᐁᑯᑕ ᐋᑳᐧ ᒋᐱᐢᑳᔨᐣ.

ᐋᐢᑲᐤ ᐄᐧᐸᐨ ᒫᓇ ᑮ ᑲᐃᐧᓯᒧᐊᐧᐠ ᐁᑲᐧ ᐄᐧᐸᐨ ᐁ ᐊᐧᓂᐢᑳᒋᐠ. ᐁᑯᓯ. ᐁ ᐯᑯᐸᔨᒋᐠ ᐁᑲᐧ, ᐋᓴᐩ ᒦᓇ ᓄᐦᑖᐃᐧᐩ ᑮᑭᓭᐹ ᐁ ᐴᓂ ᒦᒋᓱᒋᐠ, ᐋᓴᐩ ᒦᓇ ᓈᑕᑫᐧᐤ, ᒥᐢᒉᐟ ᐊᔨᐢ ᒫᓇ ᐃᐧᔭ ᑮ ᐊᑯᑖᐊᐧᐠ ᑖᐸᑳᐧᓇ, ᐋᐧᐳᓴᐧ ᐁ ᑖᐸᑲᐧᒪᐋᐧᒋᐠ.

ᐁᑯᓯ, ᑭᓀᐧᓰᐢ ᐃᑌᔨᐦᑎᐤ. ᐁᑯᓯ, ᐁᐧᐦᒋᑕᐃᐧ ᑖᐦ ᑖᐸᑳᐧᑌᐤ ᐋᐧᐳᓴᐧ ᐁᑲᐧ ᐊᓂᒪ ᐃᑕ ᑳ ᑮ ᑖᐸᑲᐧᒪᐋᐧᐟ ᐊᓂᐦᐃ ᓯᐦᑯᓴ ᐅᑎᐦᑕᑦ ᐁᑲᐧ. ᒪ ᑮᑲᐧᐩ, ᐁᑯᑕ ᐋᐧᐳᓴᐧ ᐁ ᑮ ᑖᐸᑳᐧᑖᐟ ᐁᓴ ᐊᓂᒪ ᐃᑕ ᑳ ᑮ ᐅᓰᐦᑕᒪᐋᐧᐟ ᐊᓂᐦᐃ ᓯᐦᑯᓴ, ᐃᑕ ᑳ ᑮ ᑖᐸᑲᐧᒪᐋᐧᐟ ᓯᐦᑯᓴ, ᐁᑯᑕ ᑳ ᑮ ᑖᐸᑳᐧᑖᐟ ᐋᐧᐳᓴᐧ ᐊᓂᐦᐃ. ᐊᔨ, ᑮ ᒫᒪᐢᑳᑕᒪᐧᐠ ᐊᓂᐦᐃ ᐅᐢᑌᓴ, ᐅᓰᒥᓴ ᐁ ᐋᒋᒧᐢᑕᐋᐧᐟ, « ᐁ ᑖᐯᐧᔮᐣ, » ᐃᑘᐤ. *[ᐁ ᐹᐦᐱᓯᐟ]*

ᐦᐋᐤ, ᐁᑯᓯ ᐁᑲᐧ ᒦᓇ ᐊᐊᐧ ᑯᑕᐠ ᐁᑲᐧ ᓄᐦᒑᐄᐧᐢ ᐄᐧᐢᑕ, ᐋᒋᒧᐤ.

« ᐦᐋᐤ, ᓂᒌᒥᐣ, ᓃᐢᑕ ᑭᑲ ᐋᒋᒧᐢᑖᑎᐣ, ᐁ ᑖᐯᐧᔮᐣ ᒦᓇ ᐆᒪ, » *[ᐁ ᐹᐦᐱᓯᐟ]* ᐃᑘᐤ, « ᐁ ᑮ ᐃᐢᐸᔨᐠ. ᐊᐊᐧ ᑮᑎᑦ, *« ᓂᑮ ᓈᓯᐋᐧᐣ, »* ᐃᑘᐤ, *« ᓲᓂᔮᐤ ᐅᑭᒫᓈᕽ. ᐦᐋᐤ, ᓂᑮ ᒥᔨᑲᐃᐧᐣ, ᐁᑲᐧ ᒫᓇ ᑳ ᒥᔨᑲᐃᐧᔭᕽ ᑕᐦᑐ ᐲᓯᑦ, ᐊᓈᐢᑳᓀᑭᓇᐧ ᓂᑮ ᒥᔨᑲᐃᐧᐣ ᐁᑲᐧ ᒦᓇ ᑳ ᐊᓴᒥᑲᐃᐧᔭᕽ, ᑯᐦᑰᓯᐃᐧᔨᐣ, »»* ᐃᑘᐤ. « ᐁᑯᓯ ᐁ ᑕᑯᐦᑕᑖᔮᐣ ᐁᑲᐧ ᑮᑎᑦ ᐊᐊᐧ ᐃᑘᐤ: *« ᒪᐦᑎ ᐯᑖ ᐊᓂᒪ ᐊᓈᐢᑳᓀᑭᐣ, »* ᓂᑎᐠ, » ᐃᑘᐤ.

« ᐁᑯᓯ, ᓂᒥᔮᐤ, » ᐃᑘᐤ, «« *ᐦᐋᐤ, ᑳ ᐅᓰᐦᑕᒫᑎᐣ ᐊᔭ, ᐊᐢᑎᓴᐠ, »* ᓂᑎᐠ, » ᐃᑘᐤ. « ᐊᐧᐦᐋᐧ, « *ᑖᐯᐧ ᓂᐄᐧ ᐊᑕᒥᐦᐃᐠ, »* ᓂᑌᔨᒫᐤ, » ᐃᑘᐤ, « ᓂᑌᔨᒫᐤ, » ᐃᑘᐤ. « ᐁᑯᓯ, ᐃᐧᔨᓴᐧᐤ, » ᐃᑘᐤ, « ᐁᑲᐧ ᐁ ᑲᐢᑮᑳᐧᑖᐟ; ᐦᐋᐤ,

ᒥᐢᑕᐢᑎᓴ. « *ᐦᐋᐤ, ᐁᑯᓯ, ᓂᑲ ᑮᓲᓯᐣ ᐁᑿ,* » ᓂᑕᐩ ᐃᑖᐤ, » ᐃᑘᐤ.

« ᐁᑯᓯ ᒫᑲ ᑮᑭᓭᐹ ᐁ ᐑ ᓈᑕᑵᔮᐣ, ᓂᓯᐺᐦᑕᐦᐚᐘᐠ, » ᐃᑘᐤ. « ᐯᔭᐠ ᓂᐢᑕᑦ ᐊᓂᑕ ᑖᐸᑻᓂᐢ, » ᐃᑘᐤ, « ᑳ ᐊᑎ ᐅᑎᐦᑕᒫᐣ ᐁᑯᑕ ᐋᓴᐩ ᑳ ᑖᐸᑻᓱᐟ ... ᐚᐳᐢ ! » ᐃᑘᐤ. « ᐘᐦᐚ, ᒥᑐᓂ ᓵᐦ ᓲᐦᑫᐸᔨᐦᐅᐤ, » ᐃᑘᐤ. « ᒉᐧᐢᒥ ᐁ ᐊᑎ ᐅᑎᐦᑕᐠ ᑳ ᐸᐢᑭᐸᔨᐦᐅᐟ, » ᐃᑘᐤ. « ᐁᑯᓯ ᐁᑿ ᓂᑎᓯᐍᐱᓈᐤ ᓂᑕᐢᑎᐢ, » ᐃᑘᐤ. « ᓃᑳᐣ, ᐹᒷᔪᐢ ᓂᓃᑳᓂᐍᐱᓈᐤ, » ᐃᑘᐤ, « ᐃᑕ ᐁ ᐑ ᐱᒥᐸᔨᐟ, ᐦᐋ, ᐁᑯᑕ, » ᐃᑘᐤ, « ᒥᑐᓂ ᐱᑯ ᐁ ᓴ~ *[ᐁ ᐹᐦᐱᐟ]* ᐁ ᓴᑰᐟ ᐊᓂᐦᐃ ᓂᑕᐢᑎᓴ. ᒥᐢᑕᐦᐃ ~ ... ᑮ ᒥᓯᑭᑎᐤ ᐊᔨᐢ ᐊᓇ ᒍᑌ ᓂᑕᐢᑎᐢ, » ᐃᑘᐤ. « ᐦᐋ, ᐁᑯᑕ ᓴᑰ, » ᐃᑘᐤ. « ᐁᑯᓯ ᑳ ᐃᓯ ᒥᓇᐦᐅᔮᐣ. » *[ᐁ ᐹᐦᐱᕽ]*

ᐁᑯᓯ.

(7) ᑳ ᓅᐦᑌᐦᑲᑌᐟ ᐄᐧᓴᐦᑫᒑᕽ
[*Wilfred James Martin and Vivian Young, Moose Lake, MB*]

ᐋᐦ, ᒥᐢᑕᐦᐃ ᓅᐦᑌᐦᑲᑌᐤ ᐊᐊᐧ ᐄᐧᓴᐦᑫᒑᕽ ᐁᑳᐧᓂ ᒪ ᒣᑳᐧᐸᓃᐢᑕᐁᐧᐤ ᒪᐦᐃᐦᑲᓇ, ᐁᑳᐧᓂ ᐁ ᑮ ᓂᐸᐦᐋᐧᓂᐟ ᐁᓴ ᒨᓴᐧ. ᐋᐦ, ᓅᐦᑌᐦᑲᑌᐤ, ᒫᒍᓂᒣᐤ ᒪᐦᐃᐦᑲᓇ ᐁᑳᐧᓂ ᒫᒋ ᒪᒥᐦᒋᒧᐤ: « ᓃᓇ ᓂᒫᐊᐧᒋ ᑭᓰᐸᐦᑖᐣ ᐆᑕ ᐊᐢᑮᕽ, ᒨᓇ ᓈ ᑭᐄᐧ ᑲ ᑯᒋᐢᑳᓯᓈᐋᐧᐤ? » ᐃᑌᐧᐤ ᐄᐧᓴᐦᑫᒑᕽ. ᑲᓇᐋᐧᐸᒣᐊᐧᐠ ᐆᑭ ᒪᐦᐃᐦᑲᓇᐠ, ᓇᐊᐧᐨ ᐱᑯ ᒪᒉᓂᒣᐊᐧᐠ ᐄᐧᓴᐦᑫᒑᐦᑲᐧ. « ᑭᐄᐧ ᑲ ᑯᒋᐢᑳᓯᓈᐋᐧᐤ ᓈ? » ᐃᑌᐧᐤ ᐄᐧᓴᐦᑫᒑᕽ. « ᒪᐦᑎ ᐊᐄᐧᓇ ᐆᑕ ᓃᑳᐣ ᑫ ᑕᑯᐸᐦᑖᐟ, ᑲ ᐋᐧᐢᑳᓂᐸᐦᑖᓈᓇᐤ ᐆᒪ ᓵᑲᐦᐃᑲᐣ ᐁ ᐃᐢᐲᐦᒑᐠ, » ᐃᑌᐧᐤ.

ᐁᑳᐧᓂ ᐊᐢᐱᓇᐠ. « ᑲᐧᔭᐢᐠ, » ᐃᑌᐧᐤ ᐄᐧᓇ ᐊᐊᐧ ᐃᐢᐲ ᐱᒥᐸᐦᑖᐊᐧᐠ ᒪᐦᐃᐦᑲᓇᐠ ᐁᑲᐧ ᐆᑌ ᐃᓯ ᐄᐧᐢᑕ ᐄᐧᓴᐦᑫᒑᕽ. ᒨᓇ ᒦᓇ ᐄᐧᓇ ᐋᐧᓇᐤ ᐃᐢᐸᐦᑖᐤ ᐊᐊᐧ ᐄᐧᓴᐦᑫᒑᕽ ᑳᓰᐸᓂᐦᐅᐤ. ᐊᔭ ᒧᐢᒋ ᑲᓇᐋᐧᐸᒣᐤ ᐊᓂᐦᐃ ᒪᐦᐃᐦᑲᓇ ᐃᐢᑯ ᐁᑳ ᑳ ᓅᑯᓯᓂᐟ ᐁᑳᐧᓂ ᐯ ᐋᓴ ᑮᐁᐧᐤ, ᐯ ᐋᓴ ᑮᐁᐧᐸᐦᑖᐤ. ᑭᑕᒣᐧᐤ ᐊᓂᐦᐃ ᐊᔭᐦᐋᐊᐧ ᒨᓴᐧ.

ᐋᐦᐋ, ᑳ ᐯ ᑕᑯᐸᐦᑖᒋᐠ ᐊᓂᑭ ᒪᐦᐃᐦᑲᓇᐠ, ᐁᑯᑌ ᐊᓇ ᐄᐧᓇ ᐊᐢᐸᒋᑳᐸᐃᐧᐤ ᐄᐧᓴᐦᑫᒑᕽ ᒥᐢᑎᑯᕽ ᐁ ᐋᐧᐃᐧᓭᐢᑯᓄᐟ, ᐁ ᑮᐢᐳᐟ. ᐹᐦᐱᐦᐁᐤ ᐆᐦᐅ ᒪᐦᐃᐦᑲᓇ ᐊᔭᐤ ᐁ ᐯ ᑕᑯᐸᐦᑖᓂᐟ, ᐁᑳᐧᓂ ᐁ ᑮ ᑭᑕᒫᐧᐟ ᐊᓂᐦᐃ ᒨᓴᐧ.

ᐁᑳᐧᓂ ᐋᓴᐩ.

(8) ᐄᐧᓴᐦᑫᒑᕽ ᐁ ᑮ ᐄᐧᑭᐦᑐᐟ

[*Annabelle Sanderson, Moose Lake, MB*]

ᑲᐧᔭᐢᐠ ᐁᑎᑫᐧ ᐊᐊᐧ ᑮ ᐊᔨᐤ ᑮ ᓈᐯᐃᐧᐤ ᐄᐧᓴᐦᑫᒑᕽ, ᐁᑳᐧᓂ ᐁᑎᑫᐧ ᒦᓇ ᑮ ᐊᑎ ᐊᐩ ᐃᐢᐸᓂᓂᐤ ᑕ ᐊᔮᐟ ᑕ ᐄᐧᑭᐦᑐᐟ. ᐁᑳᐧᓂ ᑮ ᐄᐧᑭᐦᑐᐤ, ᓃᓱ ᐁᓴ ᑮ ᐊᔮᐁᐧᐤ, ᑮ ᓃᓯᓂᐊᐧ ᐅᑖᓂᓴ. ᑭᒉᐧᐢ ᒫᑲ ᐁᑎᑫᐧ ᐊᓂᒪ, ᐁᑳᐧᓂ ᐁᑎᑫᐧ ᑳ ᐃᑖᐟ ᐊᔭᐦᐋᐊᐧ ᐄᐧᑭᒫᑲᓇ, « ᓈᓂᑕᐤ ᐃᓯ ᓂᐱᔮᓂ, » ᐃᑌᐧᐤ ᐁᓴ, « ᓃᓇ ᓃᑳᐣ, ᓂᐢᑕᑦ ᓈᐯᐤ ᐅᑎᐦᑎᑯᐘᑯ, ᑲ ᒦᓈᐤ ᐆᐦᐃ ᐅᒥᓯᒫᐊᐧ, ᑭᑖᓂᓯᓇᐊᐧ ᑕ ᐄᐧᑭᒫᐟ, » ᐃᑌᐧᐤ ᐁᓴ. « ᐁᑳᐧᓂ ᓃᓇ ᐃᓇ ᒫᐧ-ᓂᑕᑌᐧᓂᑌᐣ ᑭᒉᐧᐢ ᑕ ᐱᒫᑎᓯᔮᐣ, » ᐃᑌᐧᐤ ᐁᓴ ᐄᐧᓴᐦᑫᒑᕽ. ᐦᐋᐤ, ᐁᑳᐧᓂ ᐁᓴ ᑖᐯᐧ ᐁᑯᑕ ᐊᓂᒪ ᑳ ᐊᔮᒥᐠ, ᑫᑕᐦᑕᐁᐧᐣ ᐁᓴ ᑲ ᐋᐦᑯᓯᐟ ᐄᐧᓴᐦᑫᒑᕽ, ᐁᑳᐧᓂ ᐁᑎᑫᐧ ᐴᓂ ᐱᒫᑎᓯᐤ.

ᐁᑳᐧᓂ ᐁᑎᑫᐧ ᐆᐦᐅ ᑳ ᐸᒥᓈᒋᐠ ᐁᑲᐧ ᐊᔭᐦᐋᐊᐧ ᐅᑑᐹᐹᐋᐧᐊᐧ ᐆᑯ ᐃᐢᑫᐧᐊᐧᐠ. « ᐋᐦ ᐊᔨᓯ, ᑖᐯᐧ ᑭᑎᒫᑭᓯᐤ ᑭᐹᐹᓇᐤ. » ᐁᑳᐧᓂ ᑳ ᐋᐧᐸᐦᑕᐦᑭᐠ ᐅᑖᐸᒥᐦᑖᐃᐧᓂᓂᐤ, « ᐁᑲᐧ ᐊᓂᒪ ᐁᑎᑫᐧ ᑳ ᓂᐸᐦᐃᑯᐟ ᑭᐹᐹᓇᐤ, ᒪᓂᓭᑖᐣ, » ᐁᑌᐧᐤ ᐁᓴ. ᒣᐧᐦᒋ ᐁᑯᑕ ᐁᓴ ᐃᑌᐧᐤ ᐄᐧᓴᐦᑫᒑᕽ, « ᑳᐃᐧᓇ, ᐁ ᐄᐧ ᐋᐸᒥᐦᑖᐟ. » *[ᐹᐦᐱᓯᐤ]*

ᐁᑳᐧᓂ ᐁᑎᑫᐧ ᐁᑯᓯ ᑮ ᐃᓯ ᐊᔮᐁᐧᐊᐧᐠ ᐊᐘᐦᐆ ᐊᓂᐢ ᑳ ᑮ ᐃᓯ ᓈᓇᐦᐋᐧᒥᐠ ᐃᓂᓂᐊᐧ, ᑌᓯᐱᒥᑲᓂᕽ ᑳ ᑮ ᑌᐦᑕᐢᑖᒥᐠ ᒥᔭᐤ ᐁᑲᐧᑐᐊᐧ ᐁᑎᑫᐧ ᑮ ᑌᐦᑕᒉᐊᐧᐠ ᐆᐦᐅ. ᐁᑳᐧᓂ ᐁᑎᑫᐧ ᐁᑯᑕ ᑮ ᑲᐃᐧᓯᒍᓇᐦᐋᐤ ᐊᓇ ᐁ ᓂᐱᐟ. ᐁᑳᐧᓂ ᐁᑎᑫᐧ ᐄᐧᐦᑳᑕᐤ ᑮ ᐊᐧᓂᐢᑳᐤ, ᐯ ᓯᐯᐧᐦᑌᐤ. ᐋᐦ, ᐁᑳᐧᓂ ᐸᐹᒥ ᐊᔮᐤ, ᐸᐹᒥ ᐊᔮᐤ, ᐁ ᑮ ᐊᑳᐋᐧᑖᐟ ᐊᓂᐦᐃ ᐅᑖᓂᓴ, ᐊᓂᐦᐃ ᐅᒥᓯᒫᐊᐧ, ᐁᑳᐧᓂ ᑳ ᑮ ᐋᐸᓂ ᑮᐁᐧᐟ.

ᐁᑳᐧᓂ ᑕᑯᓯᐣ ᓈᐯᐤ, ᐁᑳᐧᓂ ᐁᓴ ᑳ ᐃᑖᐟ ᐊᓇ ᓅᒍᑫᐧᓯᐤ, ᐊᓇ ᑳ ᑮ ᓇᑲᑎᐦᐟ, ᐄᐧᓴᐦᑫᒑᕽ ᐄᐧᑭᒫᑲᓇ, « ᐦᐋᐤ, ᓂᑮ ᐃᑎᐠ, » ᐃᑌᐤ ᐁᓴ ᐄᐧᑭᒫᑲᓇ, « ᓂᐢᑕᑦ ᓈᐯᐤ ᑕᑯᓯᐦᑭ ᑲ ᒦᓈᐤ ᐆᐦᐃ ᓂᑖᓂᓴ ᑕ ᐄᐧᑭᒫᐟ, » ᐃᑌᐧᐤ ᐁᓴ. ᐁᑳᐧᓂ ᐁᑎᑫᐧ ᑖᐯᐧ ᑮ ᐄᐧᑭᒉᐤ ᐁᓴ ᐄᐧᓴᐦᑫᒑᕽ ᐅᑖᓂᓴ.

ᐦᐋᐤ, ᐁᑳᐧᓂ ᑭᓀᐧᓰᐢ ᐁᑎᑫᐧ ᐁᑯᑌ ᑮ ᐊᔮᐤ ᐊᐊᐧ ᐁ ᐄᐧᒑᔮᒫᐟ ᐆᐦᐅ, ᐁᑳᐧᓂ ᐁᑎᑫᐧ ᐯᔭᑳᐧᐤ ᐁ ᑫᑭᓴᐹᓂᐠ ᐄᐧᐸᐨ ᐊᐧᓂᐢᑳᐤ ᐊᔭᐦᐋᐊᐧ ᓅᒍᑫᐧᓯᐤ ᐊᓇ. ᐁᑯᑕ ᒫᑲ ᐄᐧᓴᐦᑫᒑᕽ ᐊᔮᐤ ᑳ ᒧᓴᑎᓭᐦᑳᐧᒥᐟ ᐁᓴ, ᐦᐋᐩ, ᓴᒫᐠ ᐁᓴ ᓂᓯᑕᐃᐧᓇᐁᐧᐤ ᐊᓇ ᓅᒍᑫᐧᓯᐤ ᐊᓂᐦᐃ ᐄᐧᑭᒫᑲᓇ, ᐅᓈᐯᒪ ᐊᓂᐦᐃ. « ᐦᐋᐩ, ᐁᐊᐧᑯ ᐁᒋ ᐊᐊᐧ ᑳ ᐃᑕᐦᑲᒥᑭᓯᐟ ᐄᐧᓴᐦᑫᒑᕽ, » ᐃᑌᐧᐤ ᐁᓴ. ᓅᒋᐦᐁᐤ ᐁᓴ ᐁᑯᑕ, ᐊᑎ ᐊᐧᓇᐄᐧ ᐸ ᐸᑲᒪᐦᐁᐧᐤ.

ᐁᑳᐧᓂ, ᐃᓂᑯᕽ ᒥᐢᑕᐦᐃ ᐁ ᑮ ᐯ ᐃᑕᐦᑲᒥᑭᓯᐟ ᐊᐊᐧ ᐄᐧᓴᐦᑫᒑᕽ ᑲᐦᑭᓇᐤ ᑫᑳᐧᐣ ᐊᓂᒪ ᐁᑯᓯ ᐊᑎ ᐃᐢᐸᓂᐤ ᐆᑕ ᐊᐢᑮᕽ.

(9) ᐑᓴᐦᑫᒑᕽ ᐅᒥᑭᕀ ᒦᒋᐤ

[Mary Louise Rockthunder, Piapot First Nation, SK]

ᐯᔭᑿᐤ ᐁᓴ ᐑᓴᐦᑫᒑᕽ ᐁ ᐸ ᐱᒧᐦᑌᐟ, ᐁ ᐱᒧᐦᑌᐟ ᐑᓴᐦᑫᒑᕽ. ᐘᐦᐚ ᐦᐊᕀ, ᒥᑐᓂ ᐁᓴ ᐅᐦᑯᒪ ᐊᑳᐚᑕᒪᐍᐤ ᐁ ᓈᐦ ᓇᐘᒌᔨᐟ ᐋᒪ ᐊᔨ, ᑳᐦᑫᐘᐠ. ᐘᐦᐚ, ᓅᐦᑌ ᒦᒋᐤ ᐁᓴ, ᒨᕀ ᒫᑲ ᑮ~ ..., ᒥᓯ ᒥᐢᑎᔨᓂᐤ ᐊᔨᐢᐠ ᒥᓯ ᑭᓴᔨᓂᐤ ᐊᐘ ᐑᓴᐦᑫᒑᕽ, ᒨᔭ ᐑ ᐊᓴᒥᐠ ᐅᐦᑯᒪ. ᐘᐦᐚ, ᒥᑐᓂ ᓅᐦᑌᐦᑲᑌᐤ. ᐋᐦ, ᐁᑯᓯ ᓇᑲᑌᐤ ᐆᐦᐃ ᐅᐦᑯᒪ. ᐋᐤ ᐸᐹᒧᐦᑌᐤ. ᑮ ᐱᒧᐦᑌᐢᑭᐤ ᐊᔨᐢ ᐊᐘ ᐑᓴᐦᑫᒑᕽ. ᐘᐦᐚ, ᒥᑐᓂ ᓅᐦᑌᐦᑲᑌᐤ. ᐘᐦᐚ ! ᐅᑭᓂᔭ ᐁᓴ ᑳ ᐚᐸᒫᐟ, ᒥᑐᓂ ᐁ ᒫᐦ ᒥᐦᑯᓯᔨᐟ, ᐁᑯᓂ ᐁᓴ ᐁᑿ ~, ᓅᐦᑌᐦᑲᑌᐤ. ᐁᑯᓂ ᐁᓴ ᐁᑿ ᐅᑭᓂᔭ ᐆᐦᐃ ᒣᑐᓂ ᒥᓯ ᒧᐍᐤ. ᒥᑐᓂ ᐅᑎ.

« ᐊᐦᐋᑦ, ᓂᓰᒥᑎᐠ, ᒥᑐᓂ ᓂᑮᐢᐳᐣ ᐁᑿ. ᑖᓂᓯ ᐆᒪ ᐁ ᐃᓯᔨᐦᑳᓱᔦᐠ? »

« ᐋᐦ, ᐅᑭᓂᔭᐠ. »

« ᐋᐦᐊ, ᐁᑯ ᒌ ᐱᑯ? ᐅᐦᒋᑕᐤ ᑳ ᐊᔨᓯᔨᓃᐏᕽ ᓈᐦ ᓃᓱᐏᐦᑳᓱᓈᓂᐏᐤ, ᓇᒨᔭ ᓇᔦᐢᑕᐤ ᐅᑭᓂᔭᐠ, ᓂᓰᒥᑎᐠ, ᑕ ᑮ ᐃᓯᔨᐦᑳᑎᓱᔦᐠ. »

ᐯᔭᐠ ~, ᐘᐚᓀᔨᐦᑕᒷᐠ ᐁᓴ ᐆᑭ ᐆᑭ ᐅᑭᓂᔭᐠ ᑖᓂᓯ ᑕ ᐃᓯᔨᐦᑳᑎᓱᒋᐠ. ᐅᒥᓯ ᐁᓴ ᐯᔭᐠ ᐊᐘ ᑳ ᐃᑘᐟ ᒥᓲᑭᓂᕀ ᐊᐘ, « ᐋᐦ, ᓂᐢᑌᓴ, ᐅᑫᔭᑭᒥᐢᑫᓰᓴᐠ ᓂᑎᑲᐏᓈᐣ. » *[ᐹᐦᐱᓈᓂᐘᐣ]*

« ᐋᐦᐋ, ᐘᐦᐚ, ᑖᐻ ᑭᒫᔨᐦᑳᓱᓈᐚᐤ ! »

« ᐋ, ᐊᓂᒪ ᑳ ᒥᓯ ᒧᐏᔮᕽ, ᑳ ᒥᓯ ᒦᒋᓱᔭᐣ, ᐊᑎ ᐘᔭᐑᔭᓂ ᐆᒪ ᑭᑲ ᒫᔨᑑᑖᑯᐣ ᐊᓂᒪ ᐆᑌ *[ᐁ ᐃᓯᓂᐢᑫᐟ]*. ᒣᑐᓂ ᑭᑲ ᒥᓯ ᑫᔭᑭᓯᐣ. »

« ᐋᐦ, ᓂᑕᑭᓴ ᐁᑎᑶ ᐆᑭ ᐅᑫᔭᑭᒥᐢᑫᐦᐃᐍᓰᓴᐠ. » ᓯᐻᐦᑌᐤ, ᐱᒧᐦᑌᐤ.

ᐘᐦᐚ ! ᓅᒪᑫᓰᐢ ᐁᓴ ᐁ ᐊᑎ ᐊᔮᐟ. ᐘᐦᐚ, ᑳ ᑳᐦ ᑫᔭᑭᓯᐟ ᐆᑌ *[ᐹᐦᐱᓈᓂᐘᐣ]*, ᐱᔨᐢᐠ ᐁᓴ ᐲᑯᐱᑕᑦ ᐆᒪ ᐆᑌ ᐆᒪ ᐃᑌ ᐊᓂᒪ ᑳ ᐘᔭᐑᐟ *[ᐹᐦᐱᓈᓂᐘᐣ]*. ᐱᒧᐦᑌᐤ.

ᐘᐦᐚ ! « ᐘᐦᐚ, ᓅᐦᑯᑦ ᐆᑕ ᑳ ᐱᒥ ᐊᓭᑎᐢᑭᐟ, ᐁᐘᑯ ᑳ ᑮ ᐊᑳᐚᑕᒪᐘᐠ ᑳᐦᑫᐘᐠ. » ᐊᑎ ᒫᑖᐦᐁᐤ ᐆᐦᐃ, ᐏᔭ ᐆᒪ ᑳ ᒫᑖᐦᐃᓱᐟ *[ᐹᐦᐱᓯᓈᓂᐘᐣ]*. ᑳ ᐹᐢᑌᔨᐠ ᐁᓴ ᑳᐦᑫᐘᑯᐢ. ᐸᑯᓀᔮᔨᐤ ᐆᑕ. ᐊᑎ ᐅᑎᓇᑦ. « ᐁᐦᐋᐦᐊ, ᓅᐦᑯᑦ ᐁᓴ ᑳᐦ ᐊᑎ ᐸᑎᓇᕽ ᐅᑳᐦᑫᐘᑯᒥᐢ, ᐁᐘᑯ ᑳ ᑮ ᐊᑳᐚᑕᒪᐘᐠ. » ᐊᑎ ᐅᑎᓇᑦ ᐁᓴ ᐊᐘ ᐑᓴᐦᑫᒑᕽ ᐁᑿ ᐁ ᐊᑎ ᒦᒋᐟ ᐁᑿ ᐆᒪ. ᐘᐦᐚ, ᒣᑐᓂ, ᒣᑐᓂ ᐊᑎ ᑮᐢᐸᐤ.

ᑫᑕᐦᑕᐍ ᐁᓴ ᐱᓭᓰᓴ, « ᐑᓴᐦᑫᒑᕽ ᐅᒥᑭᐩ ᒦᐄᐄᒥᐤ ! » *[ᐹᐦᐱᓈᓂᐘᐣ]* ᑳ ᐃᑙᔨᐟ ᐁᓴ. « ᐑᓴᐦᑫᒑᕽ ᐅᒥᑭᐩ ᒦᐄᐄᒥᐤ ! »

« ᐚ, ᓂᓰᒥᑎᐠ, ᑖᓇᑕ ᐃᑕ ᐑᓴᐦᑫᒑᕽ ᐅᒥᑭᐩ ᑫ ᒦᒋᐟ. ᓅᐦᑯᑦ ᐆᒪ ᐅᑳᐦᑫᐘᑯᒥᐢ ᑳ ᒦᒋᔮᐣ. »

ᐚ, ᐋᐦᒋ ᐱᑯ ᓈᐦ ᓂᑲᒧᐘᐠ ᐆᑭ ᐱᓭᓰᓴᐠ ᑳ ᐊᑎ ᓂᓯᑕᐏᓇᕽ ᐁᓴ ᐆᒪ ᐆᑌ ᐃᑌ ᑳ ᐆᐦ ᐘᔭᐑᕽ ᐁ ᐚᑎᐘᐣ~, ᐊᔨ, ᓇᐘᒋᑯ ᐁ ᐅᓵᐚᐠ ᐆᒪ ᐁᐘᑯ ᐊᓂᒪ

ᑳ ᐊᑎ ᐸᐦᑭᐦᑎᑖᐟ ᐁᓴ ᐆᒪ ᐆᐦᐃ ᐅᑭᓂᔭ ᐅᓈᐨ ᐁ ᑮ ᑭᔭᑭᓯᐟ. *[ᐹᐦᐱᓈᓂᐊᐧᐣ]* « ᐊᐧᐦᐋᐧ ! ᐁ ᑖᐯᐧᒥᐠ ᐁᓴ ᐆᑭ ᓂᓰᒪᐠ. ᐁᒋᑲ ᐆᒪ ᑖᐯᐧ ᓂᒥᑭᐩ ᑳ ᒦᒋᔮᐣ. » *[ᒥᓯ ᐹᐦᐱᓈᓂᐊᐧᐣ, ᐋᐧᐢᑕ ᐹᐦᐱᐤ]*

ᐁᑯᓯ ! ᐦᐋ, ᐦᐋᐨ ! ᐁᑯᓯ ᒫᓇ ᑮ ᐊᐩ ᐃᓯ ᐋᑕᔫᐦᑳᓂᐃᐧᐤ, ᐁᐊᐧᑯ ᐯᔭᐠ. ᑖᓂᒥᔭᑯᕽ ᑕ ᐲᑭᐢᑫᐧᔮᐣ?

[ᑮᐦᑖᐧᐨ ᐊᐊᐧ ᐹᐦᐱᐤ] « ᐄᐧᓴᐦᑫᒫᕽ ᐅᒥᑭᐩ ᒦᐄᐄᒋᐤ ! »

wawiyatācimowinisa
Funny Little Stories

(1)

tānisi ōma ē-itwēhk? / How Is It Said?

otācimow ēkwa omasinahikēw / Storyteller and Writer:

Guy Albert

nēhiýāwiw / a Plains Cree man
ýēkawiskāwikamāhk ē-ohcīt / from Ahtahkakoop First Nation, SK
nēmitanaw-ayinānēwosāp ē-itahtopiponēt / 48 years of age

On October 3, 2004, Guy Albert recorded himself telling this story as originally told to him by his mother, Flora Albert. Guy then made an initial transcription and translation of the tape as a project for the CREE 410 (Seminar in Cree Phonology) course taught by Arok Wolvengrey in the Fall term of 2004 at the First Nations University of Canada.

Guy begins the story quoting the original storyteller, but does not maintain this once the characters within the story begin speaking and must themselves be quoted. Therefore, the earlier indications of quotation ("*itwēw*," etc.) referring to the original storyteller are presented in smaller print and offset from the main text by brackets.

(1) tānisi ōma ē-itwēhk?

niwī-ācimon ōma nīsta ē-kī-isi-pēhtamān kayāsēs ē-kī-ācimot nikāwiy ōtē kistapinānihk itē kā-wīkit.

ēsa awa pēyakwāw, (awa itwēw), ōki nīso nōcikwēsiwak, (itwēw), ōtē kīwētinohk nānitaw, (itwēw), ayi, ay-apiwak mīcisowikamikohk, (itwēw), ē-ma-minihkwēcik pihkahtēwāpoy ēkwa ē-ma-mīcisosicik, (itwēw). ēkwa ēkota wīsta nētē matwē-ay-apiw awa kotak nāpēw, (itwēw), wīsta ē-ma-mīcisot, (itwēw).

kētahtawē ēsa ē-matwē-tēpwātāt osīkinikēwa, omisi ēsa kā-itāt: *"Hey waitress, could you please bring me some yam?"* matwē-itwēw ēsa.

mitoni ēsa kā-misi-pāhpipaẏit awa pēyak nōcikwēsiw ē-tōskināt ē-wīhtamawāt wīcēwākana, "īhī, nicāhkos, kipēhtawāw cī ana nāpēw?" itwēw. "namōẏa ana ahpō ē-kaskihtāt kwēyask *cham* ka-itwēt," ēsa itēw.

ēkosi ōma ēkota ē-kipihtik ōma nitācimon.

(1) How Is It Said?

I am going to tell this story the way I heard it quite a while ago told by my mother in Prince Albert where she lives.

Once upon a time, (she said), these two old ladies (she said) from somewhere up north, (she said), ah, they were sitting in a restaurant (she said) as they were drinking coffee and having a bite to eat (she said). And there was also another one, a man, sitting close by (she said) and he too was eating (she said).

Suddenly this man calls out to the waitress and he says to her, “Hey waitress, could you please bring me some yam?” he said quite audibly.

Well, this one old lady started laughing tumultuously as she poked her friend telling her, “Good grief, my sister-in-law, did you hear that man,” she exclaimed. “He can’t even say ‘cham’?”

This is where this story of mine ends.

CĀM

(2)

kīkwāy ana kīkway? / What Is That Thing?

otācimow ēkwa omasinahikēw / Storyteller and Writer:

Doreen Martell

nēhiýawiskwēwiw / a Plains Cree woman
sihkihp-sākahikanihk ē-ohcīt / from Waterhen Lake First Nation, SK
niyānanomitanaw nikotwāsosāp ē-itahtopiponēt / 56 years of age

During the Winter term of 1998, Doreen Martell wrote down the following story, as she had heard it told on her home reserve, as an assignment for a Cree course taught by Dr. Ahab Spence at the Saskatchewan Indian Federated College. This story, as edited by Arok Wolvengrey, was first printed in the newsletter of the Cree Language Retention Committee (CLRC), *ahkami-nēhiýawētān* 2.2:22 (1998) and is reprinted here with the permission of both Doreen and the CLRC.

(2) kīkwāy ana kīkway?

pēyakwāw ēsa awa nēhiýaw nāsiwēw ispī nistam mōniyāwak kā-takohtēcik. nitawi-pīhtokwēw ēsa nīmihitowikamikohk.

kētahtawē kā-otināt awa pēyak nāpēw kīkwaya, mētoni ēkwa ēkota pāh-pīmihtawakēnēw, ē-māh-mōskopitāt, "dēng, dēng, dēng, īīk! dēng, dēng, dēng, īīk!"

ēkosi ēsa ē-pōni-pīmihtawakēnāt kā-otinahk ēsa miscikos ē-misi-nōcihāt. aýiwāk misi-mātoýiwa ōhi kīkwaya. kā-pasikōpahtācik ēsa ōki mōniyāwak ē-māci-nōtinitocik.

"nīsta awa pēyak nōcikwēsiw nipē-otihtinik, mētoni nimisi-pakamahwāw ēkosi nitapasīn."

(2) What Is That Thing?

Once, when the Whitemen had first arrived, this one Cree man went looking for supplies. He went and entered this dance-hall.

Right then this one man grabbed something, and he was really twisting its ears, and, pulling away at it, making it howl, "Daing, daing, daing, eek! Daing, daing, daing, eek!"

Then when he finished twisting its ears he took up this little stick and really meaned on it. This thing really cried even more and the White folks, jumping up at a run, all started to fight with one another.

"This one old woman came to grapple me too, so I really gave her a good wallop and I fled."

@#//#!!3Q
#~!!!!!!

(3)

kīkwāy ana? / What Is That?

otācimow ēkwa omasinahikēw / Storyteller and Writer:

Neil Sapp

nēhiýāwiw / a Plains Cree man
wāskicōsiýinīnāhk ē-ohcīt / from Little Pine First Nation, SK
nēmitanaw nīsosāp ē-itahtopiponēt / 42 years of age

In October 2004 Neil Sapp recorded himself telling this story as originally told to him by his brother, Gerry Sapp. Neil then made an initial transcription and translation of the tape as a project for the CREE 410 (Seminar in Cree Phonology) course taught by Arok Wolvengrey in the Fall term of 2004 at the First Nations University of Canada.

(3) kīkwāy ana?

kayās ōma ē-kī-ispaýik.

pēyakwāw ēsa ōki nēhiýaw mācīwiýiniwak kā-kāhcitinācik pisiskiwa. māka mōý kī-nisitawinawēwak kīkwāya awa. mitoni kāh-kitāpamēwak. "tānisi māka ka-tōtawānaw?"

"ka-kīwēhtahānaw," itwēw awa pēyak. "ka-nitaw-wāpahtihānaw maskihkīwiýiniw. kahkiýaw kīkway maskihkīwiýiniw kiskēýihtam, ahpō ē-nātawihiwēt mīna."

"ahāw." ēkosi itohtahēwak.

mētoni kāh-kitāpamēw awa maskihkīwiýiniw. "mwāc," itwēw. "namōýa wīhkāc ēkotowa nipē-nakiskawāw," itwēw. "namōý wīhkāc ēkotowa nitōh-wāpamāw," itwēw. "mistahi kīkway nikiskēýihtēn māka, māka namōýa kīkway ēkotowa. āha, māka nawac opimipaýihcikēw, kahkiýaw kīkway wiýa kiskēýihtam, itohtahihk okimāhkān wīkiwāhk."

ēkosi itohtahēwak ōhi okimāhkān wīkiwāhk. wāpahtihēwak. "kikiskēýimāw cī awa kīkway aya?" konita ē-itwēcik.

kitāpamēw. "mahti pēsiw," itwēw awa okimāhkān. "āha," itwēw. "mētoni apisīsisiw ēkwa mētoni nāpēsis ē-isinākosit. ēkwa mētoni aya ē-kinwāpēkaniýik misoy ē-ayāt iýinito-mostosak," konita ē-itwēt. "ēkwa nīso misita ē-ayāt, ēkwa nīso micihciya," itwēw. "ēkwa ē-mīhýawēkasākēsit," itwēw. "*A Cowboy* awa kā-miskawāyēk," konita ē-itwēt.

(3) What Is That?

This happened a long time ago.

This one time these Cree hunters caught an animal, but they didn't recognize what it was. They really examined it. "What will we do with it?" [they said.]

"We'll take it home," one of them said. "We'll go show the medicine man. The medicine man knows everything. He even cures the sick."

They all agreed. So they took it along.

The medicine man examined it closely. "No," he said. "I have never met up with that kind [of animal]," he said. "I have never seen that kind before," he said. "I know a lot of things, but not about that! Yes, but even moreso, the Chief, he knows everything. Take it to the Chief's place."

So they took [the animal] to the Chief's place and they showed it to him. "Do you know what this is?" they said.

He looked at it. "Bring it here," the Chief said. "Oh yes," he said. "It's really small and looks like a little boy. And it has a really long tail like a cow," he said. "It has two feet and two hands," he said. "And it has a hairy little coat," he said. "You guys found a Cowboy!" he exclaimed.

(4)

ē-sīpēkistikwānēnisot / Washing His Own Hair

otācimow ēkwa omasinahikēw / Storyteller and Writer:

Bealiqué Kahmahkotayo

nēhiýawiskwēwiw / a Plains Cree woman
wāskicōsiýinīnāhk ē-ohcīt / from Little Pine First Nation, SK
nistomitanaw nēwosāp ē-itahtopiponēt / 34 years of age

In March, 2006, Bealiqué Kahmahkotayo wrote, narrated and translated the following account of a humorous episode from her own family. This text was then analyzed as part of a class project for the CREE 411 (Seminar in Cree Morphology) course taught by Arok Wolvengrey in the Winter term of 2006 at the First Nations University of Canada. The text as originally recorded has since undergone some further minor editing by Bealiqué and Arok. This primarily involved ensuring that Bealiqué's own dialect is appropriately represented as when reductions of syllable structure (cf. *sīpēk–* vs. *kisīpēk–* "clean") are evident in her speech and in the speech of her community.

(4) ē-sīpēkistikwānēnisot

pēyakwāw ēsa mōýa kayās ōma nikāwiy awa *Mary Jane* kā-kī-itikot nohtāwiya *Horace*wa ka-sīpēkistikwānēnāt. tāpiskōc ēsa awa nohtāwiy ē-kī-kostahk nipiy, ē-kī-ay-itēýihtamān māna. ēkosi ēsa nohtāwiy kī-nitawi-sīpēkistikwānēnisow ēkospīhk ēkwa. kinwēsīs ēsa ōma ēkwa ē-nōcihtāt ta-sīpēkistikwānēnisot awa nohtāwiy. "tānisi ētikwē ē-itahkamikisit?" kī-ay-itēýihtam ēkwa awa nikāwiy. ēkosi ēsa kā-nitawāpēnawāt ōhi nohtāwiya. nikāwiy ēsa ēkwa kā-nitawi-matwēhtahikēt ēkota iskwāhtēmihk. kī-kīsi-sīpēkistikwānēw ēsa awa nohtāwiy āsay. kā-pasot ēsa nikāwiy ōma kīkway pēyakwan ē-isimākwahk kā-sīpēkāpitēhk māna. nohtāwiy ēsa awa āsay ē-kīsi-kāsīhkwēt ēkwa ē-wawēsīt. tānitē ētikwē kā-kī-wī-itohtēcik ōki ninīkihikomāwak kā-kīsikāk ēkospīhk.

ēkospīhk ēsa nītisānak ē-kī-kiyokawakik. ē-pa-pāhpiyāhk ēsa ēkwa ē-ācimostātoyāhk, ē-itācimoyāhk kīkwaya kā-kī-isi-itōtamāhk kayās aspin kā-kī-wāpamitoyāhk. nicawāsimisinānak mīna nikī-ācimānānak tānisi kā-kī-pē-ay-itahkamikisicik.

ēkosi ēsa awa nohtāwiy kā-pē-sākēwēt itē ēkota kā-ay-apiyāhk. kētahtawē ēsa kā-pasoyāhk kīkway tāpiskōc kā-sīpēkāpitēmākwahk. ēkosi ēsa ēkwa nikāwiy awa kā-otinahk anima pāhkohkwēhon nohtāwiya owēscakāsiýiwa ē-wī-pāsahk, kā-sōhkēmākwahk ēsa kīkway tāpiskōc ē-kīsi-sīpēkāpitēhoýit nohtāwiya māka ēsa owēscakāsiýiwa anita ē-miýāhtahk awa nikāwiy. kā-kakwēcimāt ēsa nohtāwiya kīkwāya ē-āpacihtāýit ka-ohci-sīpēkistikwānēnisoýit. nohtāwiy ēsa kā-itāt ōhi nikāwiya ēsa āsay ōma ē-kīsi-sāpopatāt owēscakāsa, ēkosi

(4) Washing His Own Hair

One time not too long ago my father told my mother to assist him in washing his hair. It was like my father was afraid of water, or so I thought. But I guess my father did go to wash his own hair at that time. It was quite a long time that my father was struggling with washing his hair. "Whatever is he up to?" my mother was wondering then. So she went to check up on my father. My mother went there and knocked loudly on the door. Apparently my father had already finished washing his hair. But I guess my mother smelled something that smelled just the same way as when you're brushing your teeth. My father had already finished washing his face and had started putting on his clothes. I don't know where my parents had been intending to go on that particular day.

That was the time I was visiting my younger brother. We were all laughing and telling stories to each other, telling about what we had done since we had last seen each other. Our children too, we told all about what they had been doing.

It was just then that my father came around the corner where we were sitting. Right away we could smell something that was just like the smell of toothpaste. So then my mother took the towel to dry my father's hair and the smell got stronger like my father had just finished brushing his teeth but my mother smelled it there in his hair. She asked my father what he had used to wash his hair with. My father told my mother that after he had wet his hair he ēsa piko kīkway kā-itēýihtahk nohtāwiy awa kā-sāminahk kā-mōsihtāt ēsa kīkway tāpiskōc sīpēkistikwānē-sīpēkinikan. ēwako ēsa piko kā-miskahk. ēkosi ēsa kā-misi-kispakwastāt ēkwa owēscakāsihk. wahwā, nikāwiy ēsa kā-kisiwāsit, kēkāc nohtāwiya ē-pakamahwāt. "ēkosi māna ōma ēkos īsi ē-nihtā-pāhpihikawiyān, ēkos īsi ē-nitawēyihtaman nayēstaw," kā-itāt ēsa awa nohtāwiya. nohtāwiy ēsa anima sīpēkāpitēwi-pasakwahikan ēsa anima kā-āpacihtāt.

ēkosi ēsa nohtāwiy kā-pāhpit, "ēnc! wācistakāc, ē-itēýihtamān ētikwē anima sīpēkistikwānēwi-sīpēkinikan!" kahkiýaw nipāhpinān ēkwa. ēkosi ēkwa nikāwiy kā-pīhtokwēýahkināt nohtāwiya ē-nitawi-sīpēkistikwānēnāt kwayask. nistwāw ēsa awa nikāwiy kā-sīpēkistikwānēnāt anihi nohtāwiya osām ē-sōhkēmākwaniýik sīpēkāpitēwi-pasakwahikan owēscakāsiýihk. ēkosi ēsa nikāwiy kā-nahastāt anima sīpēkāpitēwi-pasakwahikan ēkwa mīna ē-osāpamāt māna ōhi nohtāwiya kā-wī-sīpēkistikwānēýit.

wāhay. mētoni, namōýa ēwako wīhkāc niwanikiskisinān kēkāc ē-nipahi-pāhpiyāhk kahkiýaw ē-wawiyatēýihtamawāyāhkik nohtāwīnān ēkwa nikāwīnān ē-kēhtē-ayiwicik ēkwa kēyāpic ē-sākihitocik. mētoni mistahi ēkospīhk tahto-kīsikāw nikī-pāhpinān kahkiýaw ēkota kā-kiyokātoyāhk. awāsisak wīstawāw kī-pāhpiwak, ātiht mōýa kī-kiskēýihtamwak nēhiýawitotamowin.

kēyāpic māna ōma ācimowin nitātotēnān ispīhk nohtāwīnān kā-kī-kakwē-sīpēkistikwānēnisot. ēwako māna ōma miýo-ācimowin nikiskisinān kā-wī-māci-kisiwāsiyāhk ōki nītisānak!

ēkosi.

thought that anything he touched which felt something like shampoo, then he must have found it. So then he really applied it thick on his hair. Oh my, my mother got so angry she almost hit my father. "It's always like this, you like getting me laughed at, that's what you want," she told my father. It turned out that it was toothpaste that my father had used [to wash his hair].

So then my father laughed, "Why! How funny is that, I guess that I thought that it was the shampoo!" We were all laughing then. So then my mother pushed my father back in [the bathroom] taking him to wash his hair properly. Three times my mother had to wash my father's hair because the toothpaste smelled so strong in his hair. So my mother has now put away the toothpaste and she always watches my father when he's going to wash his hair.

Wow! Really, we never forget how we all nearly died laughing thinking of how cute our father and mother are and how as they are getting old they still clearly love each other. We all laughed so hard that day, and every time we visit one another there. The children were also laughing, even though some of them don't know much about Cree speech.

From time to time we still tell about that time when my father had tried to wash his own hair. We remember this heartfelt story when my siblings and I start to become angry.

That's all.

(5)

mōtha nītha *Indian* / I'm Not An Indian

otācimow / Storyteller:

Solomon Ratt

nīhithāwiw / a Woods Cree man
āmaciwīspimowinihk ī-ohcīt / from Stanley Mission, SK
niyānanomitanaw nīsosāp ī-itahtopiponīt / 52 years of age

kiskinwahamawākan / Student Transcriber

Jacyntha Laviolette

On February 13, 2006, Linguistics student Jacyntha Laviolette recorded Cree professor Solomon Ratt as he told, in the Woods Cree dialect, this story from his residential school experiences. Jacyntha then began the transcription and translation of the text as a project for the CREE 411 (Seminar in Cree Morphology) course taught by Arok Wolvengrey in the Winter term of 2006 at the First Nations University of Canada.

Arok Wolvengrey, with the help of Jean Okimāsis, then sought to complete the work on the text, before turning to the ultimate authority, Solomon himself, who filled in the final details which had escaped those less familiar with Woods Cree.

(5) mōtha nītha *Indian*

kayās māna kā-kī-awāsisīwiyān ōtī māna nikī-nitawi-ayamihcikānān kistapinānihk ikotī māna ī-nitawi-kiskinwahamākosiyāhk. tahtw-āskiy māna takwāki-pīsim kā-kī-mācihtāyāhk ī-kī-nitawi-kāh-kiskinwahamākosiyāhk ikota ōma *residential schools* kā-kī-icikātīki, ikotī kā-kī-itohtīyān, āh, *Prince Albert Indian Student Residences* kī-isithihkātīw iyakw ānima. īkwa īkota māna mistahi māna awāsisak kī-kitimākisiwak mistahi māna kī-māh-mawīhkātīwak onīkihikowāwa.

aya, mīna mistahi mīna māna nikī-mōcikihtānān māna tahtwāw kā-mātinawi-kīsikāk, īkospī māna nikī-kanawāpahtīnān, āh, cikāstīpathihcikana, *picture shows* nikī-isithihkātīnān māna. iyakoni māna, mitoni māna nikī-māh-mōcikihtānān kā-pōni-wāpahtamāhk wīth āthisk māna ī-nitawi-mītawīyāhk wathawītimihk tāpiskōc māna nīthanān, āh, *Pirates* māna nikī-mītawānān ikwa mīna *Cowboys and Indians*. ikosi māna kā-kī-isi-mītawīyāhk, ikwa ōma kā-kī-pī-is-ōhpikiyāhk ōma mitoni māna, āh ..., nikī-wīnīthimisonān, mōtha nīthanān nīhithawak ta-kī-isi-pimātisiyāhk ī-itikawiyāhk māna. ikosi māna kā-kī-is-ōhpikihikawiyāhk īkota kiskinwahamātowikamikohk.

māka piyakwāw ōma ī-kī-nitawi-kanawāpahtamāhk *Cowboys and Indians* cikāstīpathihcikan, *John Wayne* ikota mīna kā-kī-ayāt, ī-kī-nōkosit, nikī-cīhkinīn, iyakw ānima nikī-cīhkāpahtīn, nimithwīthihtīn ta-wāpahtamān, *John Wayne* ta-kanawāpamak. ikwa māna

(5) I'm Not An Indian

Long ago when I was a child we used to go to school over here, over there in Prince Albert was where we attended school. Every year we'd start in September, we'd go off to attend school there at the "residential schools" as they were called. That's where we went, it was called Prince Albert Indian Student Residences, that's what it was called. And while there the children used to be really desolate and they used to really cry for their parents, missing them a great deal.

Well, we also used to have a great deal of fun every time Saturday came around for at that time we used to watch, uh, movies, we used to call them "picture shows." Those were the ones, we really used to have fun when we finished watching them for we'd go and play outside just like we were, well, we used to play "Pirates" and also "Cowboys and Indians." That's how we used to play, and at that time as we were growing up we really used to, uh … we had a very poor opinion of ourselves. We used to be told that we shouldn't live like Cree people, that's the way we were raised there at that school.

But this one time we were going to watch this Cowboys and Indians movie, and it had John Wayne in it. I liked it, I really enjoyed watching those ones, I liked to watch those, to watch John Wayne. Then when we had finished watching kā-kī-pōni-wāpahtamāhk iyakoni aya māna nikī-nitawi-mītawānān *Cowboys and Indians* māka māna ī-kī-māwasakonitoyāhk. āh, piyakwāyihk ita *Indians* īkwa piyakwāyihk kotak *Cowboys*; ikwa māna nītha kapī māna nītha iskwīyānihk kā-kī-otinikawiyān. ikwa kītahtawī ōma ōta piyak kīsikāw nikī-ati-otinikawin, *Indians* īsa nītha ta-ayāyān. āh, namōtha nikī-cīhkīthihtīn, namōtha nītha *Indian* nikī-nōhtī-itakison ikota.

"mōtha nītha *Indian*," nikī-itwān. "namōtha niwī-*Indian*iwin!" ī-itwīyān.

"ēy," itwīw ōta piyak nāpīw kā-kī-kanawīthimikoyāhk, *supervisor* kā-kī-itiht; "ēy, tāpwī kikitimākisin ikosi ī-itīthihtaman. *Indian* athisk ōma kītha ta-kī-itīthimisoyan ikos īsi ī-itakisoyan," nikī-itikawin.

ikosi.

those ones, we used to go to play Cowboys and Indians and we'd gather ourselves together [choosing sides]. Ah, on one side were the Indians and on the other were the Cowboys. And I used to always be the one chosen last. Well, eventually on this one day I came to be chosen, and apparently I was supposed to be an Indian. Oh, I didn't like that, I really didn't want to be considered an Indian.

"I'm not an Indian," I said. "I'm not going to be an Indian," I was saying.

"Hey," said this one man who looked after us, he was called the "supervisor." "Hey, you're really pitiful thinking that way. You should think of yourself as an Indian because that's what you are," I was told.

That's all.

(6)

ē-tāh-tāpakwēhk / Snaring

otācimow / Storyteller:

Gilbert Starr

nēhiýāwiw / a Plains Cree man
acāhkosa k-ōtakohpit iyinīnāhk ē-ohcīt / from Starblanket First Nation, SK
tēpakohpomitanaw nikotwāsosāp ē-itahtopiponēt / 76 years of age

kiskinwahamawākan / Student Transcriber

Delbert Alexson

On October 16, 2004, at Starblanket First Nation, Del Alexson recorded Elder Gilbert Starr as he told these two stories of his own father and uncle's exploits snaring. Del then made an initial transcription and translation of the tape as a project for the CREE 410 (Seminar in Cree Phonology) course taught by Arok Wolvengrey in the Fall term of 2004 at the First Nations University of Canada.

(6) ē-tāh-tāpakwēhk

nika-ācimon nohtāwiy ēkwa nohcāwīs ē-kī-ācimocik mēkwāc ē-pimātisicik ōta. kī-papā-kiyokātowak aýisk kayās kisēýiniwak ōta iskonikanihk. tēpakohp ihtasiwak nohcāwīsak kiki nohtāwiy.

tahto-tipiskāw anima kī-pē-itohtēwak ē-pē-nitawāpahtocik tānisi ē-kī-isi-atoskēcik tahto-kīsikāw ēkwa ē-pimācihāwasocik wīstawāw. kī-tāpakwēwak wāposwa tahto-kīsikāw, kī-nātakwēwak ē-ohci-asamāwasocik wīstawāw. nama kīkway kī-ohci-wīcihāwak, namōýa tāpiskōc ōma anohc aýisiýiniwak ē-kihci-wīcihihcik. wiýawāw piko ē-kakwē-isi-pimācihocik ē-isi-pihkohtācik kīkway ka-mīcicik ēwakoni, ēwako piko ātawiýa kī-asamāwak sōniyāw-okimānā[hk] ohci. āh, tahto-wāpan kī-nātakwēwak, wāposwa ē-kakwē-nipahācik ēkwa nohtāwiy kī-kāh-kimotamāk ēsa, ā, sihkosa ōhi, ē-kī-mowāýit māna owāposoma.

ā, kētahtawē ēsa, " 'nitāpakwamawāw anohc awa kā-kāh-kimotamawit sihkos,' nitay-itwān," itwēw. ēkosi. cāpakwānis ēkwa osīhtāw, apisīsisiwak aýisk ōki sihkosak oscikwānis ka-miýo-tēpihtiniýik ēwakoýikohk ay-isīhtāw anima cāpakwānis. ēkosi.

takohtēw ē-otākosiniýik kā-wīhtamawāt ēkwa nikāwiya, "hāw, nōtokēsiw. nikāh-kimotamāk sihkos kē-wāpahk nika-tāpakwātāw nikī-osīhtamawāw cāpakwānis," itēw nikāwiya. ēkosi, namōýa nānitaw ay-itwēw nikāwiy. ēkosi kawisimowak āsay, āsay ēsa ēkota ākwā-cipiskāsin. āskaw

(6) Snaring

I will tell stories that my father and my uncle [his brother] told when they were alive. For the old men would go around visiting one another here on the reserve long ago. There were seven of these uncles of mine along with my father.

They came over every night to check on each other and how their work was going; every day they'd work to make a living for their children. They snared rabbits every day and they'd go check their snares in order to feed their families. They didn't receive any kind of help, it wasn't like today with the people on welfare. They had to make a living the best they could, getting something like that to eat, although they did receive some rations from the agency. Every morning they checked their snares, trying to kill rabbits, and I understand my father was repeatedly the victim of theft, there was this weasel that kept eating his rabbits.

Well, eventually, "I'd be saying, 'Today I'm setting snares for the weasel that keeps stealing from me,' " he said. And that was it. He made a little snare then because those weasels are small and for their heads to fit properly he made a small snare. Just so.

He arrived home in the evening and told my mother, "Well, old lady, a weasel keeps stealing from me and tomorrow morning I'll snare him, I made a little snare for him," he said to my mother. Well, my mother didn't have anything to say. So they went to bed already. It was already getting quite wīpac māna kī-kawisimowak ēkwa wīpac ē-waniskācik. ēkosi. ē-pēkopaýicik ēkwa, āsay mīna nohtāwiy kīkisēpā ē-pōni-mīcisocik, āsay mīna nātakwēw, miscēt aýis māna wiýa kī-akotāwak tāpakwāna, wāposwa ē-tāpakwamawācik.

ēkosi, kinwēsīs itēyihtiw. ēkosi, wēhcitawi tāh-tāpakwātēw wāposwa ēkw ānima ita kā-kī-tāpakwamawāt anihi sihkosa otihtam ēkwa. ma kīkway, ēkota wāposwa ē-kī-tāpakwātāt ēs ānima ita kā-kī-osīhtamawāt anihi sihkosa, ita kā-kī-tāpakwamawāt sihkosa, ēkota kā-kī-tāpakwātāt wāposwa anihi. ayi, kī-māmaskātamwak anihi ostēsa, osīmisa ē-ācimostawāt, "ē-tāpwēyān," itwēw. [*ē-pāhpisit*]

hāw, ēkos ēkwa mīna awa kotak ēkwa nohcāwīs wīsta, ācimow.

"hāw, nicīmin, nīsta kika-ācimostātin, ē-tāpwēyān mīna ōma," [*ē-pāhpisit*] itwēw, "ē-kī-ispaýik. awa kītim; 'nikī-nāsiwān,' itwēw, 'sōniyāw-okimānāhk. hāw, nikī-miýikawin, ēkwa māna kā-miýikawiyahk tahto-pīsim, anāskānēkinwa nikī-miýikawin ēkwa mīna kā-asamikawiyahk, kohkōsiwiýin,'" itwēw. "ēkosi ē-takohtatāyān ēkwa kītim awa itwēw: 'mahti pētā anima anāskānēkin,' nitik," itwēw.

"ēkosi, nimiýāw," itwēw, " 'hāw, k-ōsīhtamātin aya, astisak,' nitik," itwēw. "wahwā, 'tāpwē niwī-atamihik,' nitēýimāw," itwēw, "nitēýimāw," itwēw. "ēkosi, wiýiswēw," itwēw, "ēkwa ē-kaskikwātāt; hāw, mistastisa. 'hāw, ēkosi, nika-kīsōsin ēkwa,' nitay-itāw," itwēw.

dark. They used to go to bed early and get up early. That's it. Then they woke up and my father was again ready that morning, as they finished eating, again he went to check his snares for they had hung up quite a few snares in trying to snare rabbits.

He was away for quite some time. As expected, he snared quite a few rabbits and then he reached that one there where he set the snare for the weasel. There was nothing. He actually caught a rabbit in the snare there when he had made it for the weasel! Oh, his older brothers and younger brothers were amazed when he told them about it. "I'm telling the truth," he said. [he chuckles]

Ok, so now another one, this uncle of mine, he too told a story.

"All right, my brother, I too will tell you a story and I'm telling the truth," he said [chuckling], "just as it happened. This sister-in-law of yours; 'I went for supplies,' he said, 'at the agency. I received what we were always given each month. I was given blanketing and we were given some rations such as bacon," he said. "When I got back with [the supplies], your sister-in-law, she said: 'Please bring that blanketing,' she said to me," he said.

"So, I gave it to her," he said. " 'All right, I'll make you, ah, some mitts,' she told me," he said. "Oh my, 'I'll be really indebted to her,' I was thinking," he said, "I thought so of her" he said. "So she cut a pattern for them," he said, "and she sewed them, yes, some big mitts. 'All right, now I will be very warm,' I was saying," he said.

"ēkosi māka kīkisēpā ē-wī-nātakwēyān, nisipwēhtahwāwak," itwēw. "pēyak nistam anita tāpakwānis," itwēw, "kā-at-ōtihtamān ēkota āsay kā-tāpakwāsot … wāpos!" itwēw. "wahwā, mitoni sāh-sōhkēpaýihow," itwēw. "mwēsci ē-at-ōtihtak kā-paskipaýihot," itwēw. "ēkosi ēkwa nitisiwēpināw nitastis," itwēw. "nīkān, pāmwayēs ninīkāniwēpināw," itwēw, "ita ē-wī-pimipaýit, hā, ēkota," itwēw, "mitoni piko ē-sē-~ [*ē-pāhpit*] ē-sēkōt anihi nitastisa. mistahi ~ … kī-misikitiw aýis ana nētē nitastis," itwēw. "hā, ēkota sēkōw," itwēw. "ēkosi kā-isi-minahoyān." [*ē-pāhpihk*]

ēkosi.

And so it was. "In the morning, as I am going to go check my snares, I'll take them along," he said. "At that first little snare," he said, "when I was approaching there, already a rabbit was snared!" he said. "My goodness, he was really jumping around vigourously," he said, "and just as I approached him he broke loose," he said. "So then I threw my mitt," he said. "In front, before ~ I threw my mitt ahead," he said, "where he was going to run, hah! there," he said. "[chuckling] He went right inside that mitt of mine. So big ~ because that there mitt of mine was really big," he said. "Hah, he went right in there," he said. "That's how I caught my game." [laughter]

That's all.

(7)

kā-nōhtēhkatēt wīsahkēcāhk / The Hungry Wīsahkēcāhk

otācimow / Storyteller:

Wilfred James Martin

maskēkowiṅinīwiw / a Swampy Cree man
mōs-sākahikanihk ē-ohcīt / from Moose Lake, MB
nēmitanaw nēwosāp ē-itahtopiponēt / 44 years of age

kiskinwahamawākan / Student Transcriber

Vivian Young
(Wilfred omisa / Wilfred's older sister)

On February 14, 2006, Vivian Young (in Regina, SK) interviewed her younger brother (in The Pas, Manitoba) by telephone and recorded this story in their dialect of Swampy Cree. In order to work with a clearer recording, Vivian re-taped the story in her own voice, word for word as her brother had told it. This new recording was then transcribed and translated as a project for the CREE 411 (Seminar in Cree Morphology) course taught by Arok Wolvengrey in the Winter term of 2006 at the First Nations University of Canada.

(7) kā-nōhtēhkatēt wīsahkēcāhk

āh, mistahi nōhtēhkatēw awa wīsahkēcāhk ēkwāni ma-mēkwāpańīstawēw mahihkana, ēkwāni ē-kī-nipahāńit ēsa mōswa. āh, nōhtēhkatēw, māńēńimēw mahihkana ēkwāni māci-mamihcimow: "nīńa nimāwaci-kisīpahtān ōta askīhk, mōńa nā kiwī-ka-kociskāsināwāw?" itwēw wīsahkēcāhk. kanawāpamēwak ōki mahihkanak, nawac piko macēńimēwak wīsahkēcāhkwa. "kiwī-ka-kociskāsināwāw nā?" itwēw wīsahkēcāhk. "mahti awīna ōta nīkān kē-takopahtāt ka-wāskānipahtānānaw ōma sākahikan ē-ispīhcāk," itwēw.

ēkwāni aspinak. "kwayask," itwēw wīńa awa ispī pimipahtāwak mahihkanak ēkwa ōtē isi wīsta wīsahkēcāhk. mōńa mīna wīńa wāńaw ispahtāw awa wīsahkēcāhk kāsōpańihow. ayi mosci-kanawāpamēw anihi mahihkana isko ēkā kā-nōkosińit ēkwāni pē-āsē-kīwēw, pē-āsē-kīwēpahtāw. kitamwēw anihi ayah āwa mōswa.

āhā, kā-pē-takopahtācik aniki mahihkanak, ēkotē ana wīńa aspacikāpawiw wīsahkēcāhk mistikohk ē-wāwiyēskońot, ē-kīspot. pāhpihēw ōho mahihkana ayiw ē-pē-takopahtāńit, ēkwāni ē-kī-kitamwāt anihi mōswa.

ēkwāni āsay.

(7) The Hungry Wīsahkēcāhk

Well, Wīsahkēcāhk was really hungry, and he happened to meet up with some wolves, and they had apparently just killed a moose. Boy, was he hungry, and he thought to dare the wolves, so he started bragging. “I am the fastest runner here on earth. Wouldn’t you like to race against me?” said Wīsahkēcāhk. The wolves looked at him, and they were quite leery of Wīsahkēcāhk. “Are you going to race against me?” said Wīsahkēcāhk. “Let’s see who will arrive back here first, we’ll run the whole distance around the lake,” he said.

So off they went. “Perfect!” he said when the wolves ran off and Wīsahkēcāhk also took off in that direction. Wīsahkēcāhk didn’t run far though, and then he threw himself into hiding. He was just watching the wolves until they were no longer in sight and then he turned back, running back where he came from. He ate up that whole moose.

Yes, well, when those wolves arrived back at a run, there was Wīsahkēcāhk leaning up against a tree with his belly all rounded out, quite full. He laughed at the wolves as they came running back, for he had devoured the entire moose.

That’s all.

(8)

wīsahkēcāhk ē-kī-wīkihtot / Wīsahkēcāhk Got Married

otācimow / Storyteller:

Annabelle Sanderson

maskēkowiskwēwiw / a Swampy Cree woman
mōs-sākahikanihk ē-ohcīt / from Moose Lake, MB
tēpakohpomitanaw pēyakosāp ē-itahtopiponēt / 71 years of age

kiskinwahamawākan / Student Transcriber

Jeff Sanderson
(Annabelle okosisa / Annabelle's son)

On February 16, 2006, at The Pas, Manitoba, Jeff Sanderson recorded his mother telling a number of *wīsahkēcāhk* stories in her dialect of Swampy Cree. Jeff then transcribed and translated this particular story, neither the first nor the last in the story cycle, as a project for the CREE 411 (Seminar in Cree Morphology) course taught by Arok Wolvengrey in the Winter term of 2006 at the First Nations University of Canada.

(8) wīsahkēcāhk ē-kī-wīkihtot

kwayask ētikwē awa kī-ayiw kī-nāpēwiw wīsahkēcāhk, ēkwāni ētikwē mīna kī-ati-ay-ispańińiw ta-ayāt ta-wīkihtot. ēkwāni kī-wīkihtow, nīso ēsa kī-ayāwēw, kī-nīsińiwa otānisa. kinwēs māka ētikwē anima, ēkwāni ētikwē kā-itāt ayah āwa wīkimākana, "nānitaw isi nipiyāni," itwēw ēsa, "nīńa nīkān, nistam nāpēw otihtikoyēko, ka-mīńāw ōhi omisimāwa, kitānisinawa ta-wīkimāt," itwēw ēsa. "ēkwāni nīńa ińa mwāc nitatwēńitēn kinwēs ta-pimātisiyān," itwēw ēsa wīsahkēcāhk. hāw, ēkwān ēsa tāpwē ēkot ānima kā-ayācik, kētahtawēn ēsa ka-āhkosit wīsahkēcāhk, ēkwāni ētikwē pōni-pimātisiw.

ēkwāni ētikwē ōho kā-paminācik ēkwa ayah āwa otōpāpāwāwa ōko iskwēwak. "āh ayisi, tāpwē kitimākisiw kipāpānaw." ēkwāni kā-wāpahtahkik otāpacihtāwinińiw, "ēkw ānima ētikwē kā-nipahikot kipāpānaw, manisētān," itwēw ēsa. mwēhci ēkota ēsa itwēw wīsahkēcāhk, "kāwińa, ē-wī-āpacihtāt." [*pāhpisiw*]

ēkwāni ētikwē ēkosi kī-isi-ayāwēwak ayohō ańis kā-kī-isi-nānahācik ińiniwa, tēsipicikanihk kā-kī-tēhtastācik miyaw ēkwatowa ētikwē kī-tēhtańēwak ōho. ēkwāni ētikwē ēkota kī-kawisimonahāw ana ē-nipit. ēkwāni ētikwē wīhkātaw kī-waniskāw, pē-sipwēhtēw. āh, ēkwāni papāmi-ayāw, papāmi-ayāw, ē-kī-akāwātāt anihi otānisa, anihi omisimāwa, ēkwāni kā-kī-āpani-kīwēt.

ēkwāni takosin nāpēw, ēkwāni ēsa kā-itāt ana nōcokwēsiw, ana kā-kī-nakatiht, wīsahkēcāhk wīkimākana, "hāw, nikī-itik," itēw ēsa wīkimākana, "nistam nāpēw

(8) Wīsahkēcāhk Got Married

He was then a good man, Wīsahkēcāhk was, and it seems it came time for him to be, for him to marry. So then he got married, and he apparently had two, his daughters were two in number. I guess quite a long time passed and then he said to his wife, "In case I die," he said, "if I go first, the first man that comes to you, you will give him the eldest of our daughters for him to marry," he said. "Now I surely do not think that I will live very long," Wīsahkēcāhk said. Sure enough while they were staying there, Wīsahkēcāhk suddenly become ill and then he died.

Then as it happened these women prepared their father [his body]. "Oh, our poor father," [they sighed]. Then upon seeing his tool, "That must be what killed our father, let's cut it off," one said. Right away Wīsahkēcāhk said, "Don't! He's going to use it." [chuckling]

So then they prepared him in the [appropriate] way because that's the way they buried people, placing the body up on a scaffold, and I guess they placed him up on that kind. Then he was laid to rest there for he had died. Then later on he woke up and he came walking away. Well, he travelled around and around and around, desiring that daughter of his, the eldest daughter, and then he turned to head home.

Then a man arrived, so then that old woman, the one he had left, Wīsahkēcāhk's wife, said to him, "All right, he told me," she said to her spouse, "when the first man arrives takosihki, ka-mīńāw ōhi nitānisa ta-wīkimāt," itwēw ēsa. ēkwāni ētikwē tāpwē kī-wīkimēw ēsa wīsahkēcāhk otānisa.

hāw, ēkwāni kinwēsīs ētikwē ēkotē kī-ayāw awa ē-wīc-āyāmat ōho, ēkwān ētikwē pēyakwāw ē-kēkisēpāńik wīpac waniskāw ayah āwa nōcokwēsiw ana. ēkota māka wīsahkēcāhk ayāw kā-mosētiyēhkwāmit ēsa, hāāy, sēmāk ēsa nisitawinawēw ana nōcokwēsiw anihi wīkimākana, onāpēma anihi. "hāāy, ēwakw ēci awa kā-itahkamikisit wīsahkēcāhk," itwēw ēsa. nōcihēw ēsa ēkota, ati-wańawī-pa-pakamahwēw.

ēkwāni, ińikohk mistahi ē-kī-pē-itahkamikisit awa wīsahkēcāhk kahkińaw kēkwāń anima ēkosi ati-ispańiw ōta askīhk.

here, you will give him my daughter in marriage," she said. So truly it happened that Wīsahkēcāhk married his daughter.

Yes, and then for some time he was there living with them, but one morning that old woman rose from bed early. There was Wīsahkēcāhk sleeping with his buttocks exposed. Whoa! Right away the old woman recognized her partner, that it was her husband. "Hey! The whole time it's been this Wīsahkēcāhk who's been doing this!" she said. She beat him right there, she pummelled him on out the door.

And now, inasmuch as Wīsahkēcāhk had done many things in the past, all these things are now starting to happen this way here on earth.

(9)

wīsahkēcāhk omikiy mīciw / Wīsahkēcāhk Eats His Scab

otācimow / Storyteller:

Mary Louise Rockthunder

nēhiýawiskwēwiw / a Plains Cree woman
nēhiýaw-pwātināhk ē-kī-ohcīt / from Piapot First Nation, SK
ayinānēwomitanaw tēpakohposāp ē-kī-itahtopiponēt / 87 years of age

omasinahikēwak ēkwa otākaýāsiwascikēwak / Transcribers and Translators

Jean Okimāsis and Arok Wolvengrey

On March 23, 2001, at the Cree Language Retention Committee-sponsored Language Teachers' Workshop in Saskatoon, SK, Mary Louise Rockthunder narrated this *wīsahkēcāhk* story for the amusement of all in attendance. Jean had worked with Mary Louise on a number of occasions and has a number of different stories which we hope will form a larger publication in the future. For now, we would like to offer this story in memory of Mary Louise Rockthunder, who left us for the spirit world on July 2, 2004 at the age of 90.

(9) wīsahkēcāhk omikiy mīciw

pēyakwāw ēsa wīsahkēcāhk ē-pa-pimohtēt, ē-pimohtēt wīsahkēcāhk. wahwā hay, miton ēsa ohkoma akāwātamawēw ē-nāh-nawacīýit ōma ayi, kāhkēwak. wahwā, nōhtē-mīciw ēsa, mōy māka kī-~ ..., misi-mistiýiniw aýisk misi-kisēýiniw awa wīsahkēcāhk, mōýa wī-asamik ohkoma. wahwā, mitoni nōhtēhkatēw. āh, ēkosi nakatēw ōhi ohkoma. āw, papāmohtēw. kī-pimohtēskiw aýis awa wīsahkēcāhk. wahwā, mitoni nōhtēhkatēw. wahwā! okiniya ēsa kā-wāpamāt, mitoni ē-māh-mihkosiýit, ēkoni ēsa ēkwa ~, nōhtēhkatēw. ēkoni ēs ēkwa okiniya ōhi mētoni misi-mowēw. miton ōti.

"ahām, nisīmitik, mitoni nikīspon ēkwa. tānis ōma ē-isiýihkāsoyēk?"

"āāh, okiniyak."

"āha', ēko cī piko? ohcitaw kā-aýisiýinīwihk nāh-nīsowihkāsonāniwiw, namōýa nayēstaw okiniyak, nisīmitik, ta-kī-isiýihkātisoyēk."

pēyak ~, wawānēýihtamwak ēs ōk ōki okiniyak tānisi t-ēsiýihkātisocik. omisi ēsa pēyak awa k-ētwēt mis-ōkiniy awa, "āāh, nistēsē, okēýakiciskēsīsak nitikawinān." [*pāhpināniwan*]

"āhā, wahwā, tāpwē kimāýihkāsonāwāw!"

(9) Wīsahkēcāhk Eats His Scab

Once upon a time Wīsahkēcāhk was walking along, he was walking Wīsahkēcāhk was. Oh my goodness, it seems he was really craving that which his grandmother would roast, umm, *kāhkēwak* [dried meat]. Oh my, he wanted to eat it, but she didn't… Because he was a very big man, this old man Wīsahkēcāhk, his grandmother wasn't going to feed him. Gee whiz, he was really hungry. Well, so he left his grandmother. So then he wandered about. But that's Wīsahkēcāhk for you, he's always walking. My goodness, but he was very hungry. Well! Then he spotted some rose-hips, and they were really red, so those were the ones now, for he was hungry. So then he really gobbled up great quantities of those rose-hips. A great many.

"All right, my little brothers, now I'm really full. What are you called?"

"Oh, rose-hips."

"Yes, but only that? It's compulsory that, among people, there be two names, so my little brothers, you should not call yourselves by the name 'rose-hips' alone."

One ~, these here rose-hips were at a loss for what other name they had. Then this one large rose-hip spoke up saying: "Oh, elder brother, we are called Little Butt Itchers." [laughter]

"Oho, my goodness, you have a truly hideous name!"

"āā, anima kā-misi-mowiyāhk, kā-misi-mīcisoyan, ati-waýawīyani ōma kika-māýi-tōtākon anima ōtē. [*ē-isiniskēt*] mētoni kika-misi-kēýakisin."

"āāh, nitakisa ētikw ōki okēýakiciskēhiwēsīsak." sipwēhtēw, pimohtēw.

wahwā! nōmakēsīs ēsa ē-at-āyāt. wahwā, kā-kāh-kēýakisit ōtē [*pāhpināniwan*], piýisk ēsa pīkopitam ōm ōtē ōm ītē anima kā-waýawīt. [*pāhpināniwan*] pimohtēw.

wahwā! "wahwā, nohkom ōta kā-pim-āyētiskit, ēwako kā-kī-akāwātamawak kāhkēwak." ati-mātāhēw ōhi, wiý ōma kā-mātāhisot [*pāhpisināniwan*]. kā-pāstēyik ēsa kāhkēwakos. pakonēyāýiw ōta. at-ōtinam. "ēhāha, nohkom ēsa kāh-ati-patinahk okāhkēwakomis, ēwako kā-kī-akāwātamawak." at-ōtinam ēsa awa wīsahkēcāhk ēkwa ē-ati-mīcit ēkw ōma. wahwā, mētoni, mētoni ati-kīspow.

kētahtawē ēsa piýēsīsa, "wīsahkēcāhk omikiy mīīīciw!" [*pāhpināniwan*] kā-itwēýit ēsa. "wīsahkēcāhk omikiy mīīīciw!"

"wā, nisīmitik, tānita ita wīsahkēcāhk omikiy kē-mīcit. nohkom ōma okāhkēwakomis kā-mīciyān."

wā, āhci piko nāh-nikamowak ōki piýēsīsak kā-ati-nisitawinahk ēsa ōm ōtē itē k-ōh-waýawīhk

"Ah, since you ate so many of us, since you ate such a great amount, when nature calls it's going to have quite a bad effect on you over here [gestures]. You will really get very itchy."

"Aah, there's nothing to these Little Butt Itchers." He merely left and walked on.

My goodness! I guess he had been on his way for a while. Oh my, by then he kept itching over here [laughter], and eventually he tore [the scab] loose over here from where he voids [laughter]. And on he walked.

Well! "Goodness, my grandmother was leaving tracks along here, the one who's dried meat I wanted." He started tracking her, but it was himself that he was tracking [chuckling]. There [he found] some really dry *kāhkēwak*. Here it had a hole in the middle of it. He took it up. "Oh yes, my grandmother must have dropped her dried meat, the stuff I had wanted." Wīsahkēcāhk took it up and started eating it right then. Oh my, really, he started getting very full.

All of a sudden, some birds were singing, "Wīsahkēcāhk eats his owwwn scab!" [laughter]. "Wīsahkēcāhk eats his owwwn scab!"

"Whoa, my little brothers, from where might the scab come that Wīsahkēcāhk would eat? It's my grandmother's dried meat that I'm eating."

Well, nevertheless these birds kept singing and he started to recognize this from over here where one voids, the hole ē-wātiwan-~, ayi, nawaciko ē-osāwāk ōma ēwakw ānima kā-ati-pahkihtitāt ēsa ōma ōh ōkiniya osām ē-kī-kēýakisit. [*pāhpināniwan*] "wahwā! ē-tāpwēcik ēsa ōki nisīmak. ēcik ōma tāpwē nimikiy kā-mīciyān." [*misi-pāhpināniwan; wīsta pāhpiw*]

ēkosi! hā, hām! ēkosi māna kī-ay-is-ātaýōhkāniwiw, ēwako pēyak. tānimiýikohk ta-pīkiskwēyān?

[*kīhtwām awa pāhpiw*] "wīsahkēcāhk omikiy mīīīciw!"

… ah, that which he had let drop was somewhat orange and it was due to the rose-hips that he was itchy. [laughter] "Oh no! These younger brothers of mine are telling the truth. It appears that I was really eating my own scab." [great laughter; she laughs as well]

That's it. All right. That's how this sacred story is always told, this is one of them. How long should I speak?

[laughing again] "Wīsahkēcāhk eats his owwwn scab!"

Cree-English Glossary

Stem-Class Codes

INM	Indeclinable Nominal
IPC	Indeclinable Particle
IPH	Indeclinable Particle Phrase
IPN	Indeclinable Prenoun
IPV	Indeclinable Preverb
NA	Animate Noun
NDA	Dependent Animate Noun
NDI	Dependent Inanimate Noun
NI	Inanimate Noun
PR	Pronoun
PrA	Animate Pronoun
PrI	Inanimate Pronoun
VAI	Animate Intransitive Verb
VAIt	Syntactically Transitive, Morphologically *VAI*
VII	Inanimate Intransitive Verb
VTA	Transitive Animate Verb
VTI	Transitive Inanimate Verb

Please note that three additional dialect codes are used within this glossary:

pC	Plains Cree	(or ý-dialect)
sC	Swampy Cree	(or ń-dialect)
wC	Woods Cree	(or th-dialect)

For further notes on the format of this glossary, see the Introduction to this volume and/or consult the glossaries in similar works such as Ahenakew (1986, 1987b), Kā-Nīpitēhtēw (1998), or Wolvengrey (2001).

-cawāsimis- *NDA* child [e.g. *nicawāsimisinānak* "our children"; cf. *awāsis- NA*]

-cāhkos- *NDA* [female speaker only:] female cross-cousin; sister-in-law [e.g. *nicāhkos* "my (female cross-)cousin; my sister-in-law"]

-cihciy- *NDI* hand [cf. unspecified possessor form *micihciya* "hands"; cf. *micihciy NDI*]

-iyaw- *NDI* body [e.g. *miyaw* "a body"]

-īcēwākan- *NDA* companion, partner, friend [e.g. *wīcēwākana NDA* "her [obviative] companion, partner, friend"]

-īk- *NDI* home, place [sg: *-īki*; e.g. *wīkiwāhk* "at their home"; cf. *wīki NDI* "his/her home"]

-īkimākan- *NDA* his/her spouse [e.g. *wīkimākana* "his wife; her husband [obviative]"]

-ītimw- *NDA* cross-cousin of opposite gender; sister-in-law (in relation to a male); brother-in-law (in relation to a female) [e.g. *kītim* "your sister-in-law; your brother-in-law"]

-ītisān- *NDA* sibling [e.g. *nītisānak* "my siblings"]

-kāhkēwakomis- *NDI* little piece of dried meat [e.g. *okāhkēwakomis* "her little piece of dried meat"; cf. *kāhkēwakw- NI*; *kāhkēwakos- NI*]

-kāwiy- *NDA* mother [e.g. *nikāwiy* "my mother"; e.g. *nikāwiya* "my mother [obviative]"]

-mikiy- *NDI* scab [cf. *omikiy- NI*]

-mis- *NDA* older sister [e.g. *omisimāwa* "the eldest sister [obviative]"]

-nīkihikw- *NDA* parent [e.g. *onīkihikowāwa* "their parents"; sometimes *-nēkihikw-* in Plains Cree]

-ohcāwīs- *NDA* uncle, father's brother [e.g. *nohcāwīsak* "my uncles"]

-ohkom *NDA* grandmother [e.g. *nohkom* "my grandmother"; e.g. *ohkoma* "his/her grandmother"]

-ohtāwiy- *NDA* father [e.g. *nohtāwiy* "my father"; e.g. *nohtāwiya* "my father [obviative]"]

-opāpā- *NDA* dad, father [sC; e.g. *otōpāpāwāwa* "their dad [obviative]"; cf. *-pāpā-*]
-pāpā- *NDA* dad, father [sC; e.g. *kipāpānaw* "our dad"; cf. *-opāpā-*]
-scikwānis- *NDI* little head [e.g. *oscikwānis* "his little head"]
-sit- *NDI* foot [cf. unspecified possessor form *misita* "feet"; cf. *misit- NDI*]
-sīm- *NDA* younger sibling, little brother, little sister [e.g. vocative: *nisīmitik* "my younger siblings"]
-sīmis- *NDA* younger sibling, younger brother or sister [e.g. *osīmisa* "his younger sibling(s) [obviative]"]
-soy- *NDI* tail [cf. unspecified possessor form, *misoy* "tail"]
-stēs- *NDA* older brother [e.g. vocative: *nistēsē* "my older brother!"; e.g. *ostēsa* "his older brother(s) [obviative]"]
-tānis- *NDA* daughter [e.g. *otānisa* "his/her daughter(s)"; e.g. *kitānisinawa* "our daughter(s) [obviative]"]
-wāposom- *NDA* rabbit [e.g. *owāposoma* "his rabbit(s)"; cf. *wāposw- NA* + -im "possessive suffix"]
-wēscakās- *NDI* hair [e.g. *owēscakāsiýiwa* "his [obviative] hair"; cf. *-ēscakās-*]

ahām *IPC* okay, all right; well
ahāw *IPC* all right, okay; let's go
ahpō *IPC* or; even [cf. *namōýa ahpō IPH*]
akāwāt- *VTA* desire s.o., want s.o., lust after s.o. [e.g. *ē-kī-akāwātāt* "(as) he desired her"]
akāwātamaw- *VTA* covet (it/him/her) from s.o., desire something from s.o. [e.g. *akāwātamawēw* "he desires it of her"]
akotā- *VAIt* hang s.t., hang s.t. up [e.g. *kī-akotāwak* "they hung them up"]
ana *PrA* that, that one [animate proximate singular pronoun]
anāskānēkinw- *NI* blanket, blanketing; sheet, sheeting [e.g. *anāskānēkinwa* "blankets"; sg: *anāskānēkin*]
anihi *IPC* it was (that) [focus marker]
anihi *PrA* that, that one; those, those ones [animate obviative (singular or plural) pronoun]

aniki *PrA* those, those ones [animate proximate plural pronoun]
anima *IPC* it was (that) [focus marker]
anima *PrI* that, that one [inanimate singular pronoun]
ańis *IPC* because, for [sC; cf. pC: *aýis*]
anita *IPC* there
anohc *IPC* today, now
api- *VAI* sit; be at home [especially when reduplicated; e.g. *ay-apiwak* "they are sitting; they are at home"; e.g. *kā-ay-apiyāhk* "where we are sitting"]
apisīsisi- *VAI* be small, be little in size [e.g. *apisīsisiw* "he is small"; e.g. *apisīsisiwak* "they are small"]
asam- *VTA* feed s.o., feed it to s.o. [e.g. *kī-asamāwak* "they were fed"; e.g. *kā-asamikawiyahk* "which we were fed"; e.g. *wī-asamik* "s/he is going to feed him"]
asamāwaso- *VAI* feed one's children, provide food for one's children [e.g. *ē-ohci-asamāwasocik* "in order to feed their children"]
askiy- *NI* land, earth [e.g. locative: *askīhk* "in the land; on the land, on earth"]
askīhk *IPC* on earth, in the land; on the land [locative; cf. *askiy- NI*]
aspacikāpawi- *VAI* stand leaning against something [e.g. *aspacikāpawiw* "he stands leaning against (it)"]
aspin *IPC* ago; since
aspinak *IPC* away they went, they were off [sC; apparently plural form of *aspin*]
astis- *NA* mitt [e.g. *astisak* "mitts"; e.g. *nitastis* "my mitt"]
atamih- *VTA* please s.o.; make s.o. thankful [e.g. *niwī-atamihik* "she's going to make me happy; I'm going to be grateful to her"]
at-āyā- *VAI* be so, go along so [e.g. *ē-at-āyāt* "(as) s/he was going along"]
athisk *IPC* because, for [wC; cf. pC: *aýisk*, sC: *ańis*]
ati- *IPV* progressively; start to, begin to [e.g. *nikī-ati-otinikawin* "I was being chosen"; e.g. *kā-at-ōtihtamān* "when I was approaching it"; e.g. *ati-wayawīyani* "when you start going outside; when nature starts

a'calling"; e.g. sC: *kī-ati-ay-ispańińiw* "it came to pass"; e.g. sC: *ati-wańawī-pa-pakamahwēw* "she pummelled him right outside"]

atoskē- *VAI* work, do work [e.g. *tānisi ē-kī-isi-atoskēcik* "how their work was going"]

awa *IPC* it is (this) [focus marker]

awa *PrA* this, this one [animate proximate singular pronoun]

awāsis- *NA* child [e.g. *awāsisak* "children"; cf. *-cawāsimis- NDA*]

awāsisīwi- *VAI* be a child [e.g. *kā-kī-awāsisīwiyān* "when I was a child"]

awīna *PrA* who [animate proximate singular interrogative pronoun]

ay- *IPV* ongoing, continually [light reduplication of vowel- initial stems; e.g. *ay-apiwak* "they are sitting"; e.g. *nitay-itwān* "I say"; e.g. *ay-isīhtāw* "s/he makes it thus"; e.g. *kā-kī-pē-ay-itahkamikisicik* "what they had been up to"; e.g. sC: *kī-ati-ay-ispańińiw* "it came to pass"; e.g. *kī-ay-is-ātaýōhkāniwiw* "the sacred story was told so"]

aya *IPC* ah, umm; ya [hesitation particle, often used to fulfill prosodic requirements of a phrase]

ayah āwa *PrA* this here one, this previously mentioned one [sC; animate proximate singular pronoun; apparent marker of previous topic; often accompanied by a gesture; also: *ayahi awa*]

ayamihcikī- *VAI* read; attend school [wC; cf. *ayamihcikē-*; e.g. *nikī-nitawi-ayamihcikānān* "we went to attend school"]

ayā- *VAI* be, exist; be located, be there [e.g. *ta-ayāt* "for him to be"; e.g. *kā-ayācik* "where they were"; e.g. *papāmi-ayāw* "he loitered about, he stayed all over the place"; e.g. *ē-at-āyāt* "(as) s/he was going along"; e.g. *kā-kī-ayāt* "who was there"; e.g. *ta-ayāyān* "for me to be …"]

ayā- *VAIt* have s.t. [e.g. *ē-ayāt* "(as) he has it"]

ayāw- *VTA* have s.o. [e.g. *kī-ayāwēw* "he had them"]

ayētiski- *VAI* leave tracks [e.g. *kā-pim-āyētiskit* "where s/he is leaving tracks"; cf. *pimi- IPV*]

ayi *IPC* ah, umm [hesitation; can also be inflected as a verb, e.g. *kī-ayiw* "he was ahh…"]

aýis *IPC* because, for [cf. *aýisk*; sC: *ańis*]

aýisiýiniw- *NA* person, human being [e.g. *aýisiýiniwak* "people"] aýisiýinīwi- *VAI* be human, be a human being [e.g. *kā-aýisiýinīwihk* "where humans are involved; when there are people"]

aýisk *IPC* because, for [cf. *aýis*; wC: *athisk*]

ayiw *IPC* ah, umm [verbal hesitation; third person singular Independent form; cf. *ayi*]

aýiwāk *IPC* more, further

ayohō *IPC* that one there; those ones there [sC; animate obviative pronoun; apparent marker of previous topic]

ā *IPC* ah, umm [hesitation]

āā *IPC* oh; well

āāh *IPC* oh, ahh

ācim- *VTA* tell news about s.o. [e.g. *nikī-ācimānānak* "we told about them"]

ācimo- *VAI* tell a story, tell stories; tell news [e.g. *nika-ācimon* "I will tell a story"; e.g. *niwī-ācimon* "I'm going to tell a story"; *ē-kī-ācimot* "(as) s/he told a story"; e.g. *ē-kī-ācimocik* "(as) they told stories"]

ācimostaw- *VTA* tell a story to s.o., tell stories to s.o., tell news to s.o. [e.g. *kika-ācimostātin* "I'll tell you a story"; e.g. *ē-ācimostawāt* "(as) he told his story to them"]

ācimostāto- *VAI* tell news to one another, tell one another stories [e.g. *ē-ācimostātoyāhk* "(as) we tell each other the news"]

ācimowin- *NI* story; news [e.g. *nitācimowin* "my story"]

āh *IPC* oh, ahh

āh *IPC* well; ah, umm [hesitation]

āh ayisi *IPH* ahh, me; isn't it sad [a spoken "heavy sigh"]

āha *IPC* yes

āha' *IPC* yes [note: the apostrophe represents a glottal stop or glottal catch at the end, no longer common in the speech of younger Cree speakers]

āhā *IPC* oho, holy!

āhā *IPC* yes, all right then

āhci piko *IPH* still, neverthless

āhkosi- *VAI* be sick, be ill [e.g. *ka-āhkosit* "he falls ill"]

ākwā- *IPV* well on the way (in time), quite a lot [e.g. *ākwā-cipiskāsin* "it is quite dark"]

ākwā-cipiskāsin- *VII* be quite dark, be getting late
āpacihtā- *VAIt* use s.t. [e.g. *ē-wī-āpacihtāt* "(as) he's going to use it"; e.g. *ē-āpacihtāýit* "that he uses"; e.g. *kā-āpacihtāt* "that which he used"]
āpacihtāwin- *NI* tool; useful object [e.g. sC: *otāpacihtāwiniňiw* "his tool [obviative]"]
āpani- *IPV* turn back, do an about-face [e.g. *kā-kī-āpani-kīwēt* "when he turned back homewards"]
āsay *IPC* already, without delay
āsay mīna *IPH* again, already again
āsē- *IPV* in reverse, backwards [e.g. *pē-āsē-kīwēpahtāw* "he comes running back homewards"]
āskaw *IPC* sometimes, at times
ātawiýa *IPC* though, although; nonetheless, anyway
ātaýōhkē- *VAI* tell a sacred story, tell a legend [e.g. *kī-ay-is-ātaýōhkāniwiw* "the sacred story was told so"]
ātiht *IPC* some
ātot- *VTI* tell s.t., tell about s.t. [e.g. *nitātotēnān* "we tell about it"]
āw *IPC* well, all right [cf. *hāw*]
cāpakwānis- *NI* small snare [diminutive; cf. *tāpakwān-*]
cikāstīpathihcikan- *NI* movie, picture show [wC: e.g. *cikāstīpathihcikana* "movies"; cf. pC: *cikāstēpaýihcikan-*]
cipiskāsin- *VII* be a little dark, be approaching night [diminutive; e.g. *ākwā-cipiskāsin* "it is quite dark"; cf. *tipiskā- VII*]
cī *IPC* [interrogative particle; follows an element in initial, focus position to indicate a yes-no question; cf. sC: *nā*]
cīhkāpaht- *VTI* like to watch s.t., like the look of s.t., enjoy watching s.t. [e.g. wC: *nikī-cīhkāpahtīn* "I liked watching it"]
cīhkin- *VTI* enjoy s.t. [e.g. wC: *nikī-cīhkinīn* "I liked it"]
cīhkīthiht- *VTI* enjoy s.t., like s.t. [e.g. wC: *namōtha nikī-cīhkīthihtīn* "I didn't like it"; cf. pC: *cīhkēýiht-*]
ē- *IPV* that, as [marker of conjunct mode; cf. wC: *ī-*]
ēci *IPH* what is this? so this is … [cf. *ēwakw ēci awa IPH*]
ēcik ōma *IPH* and so it appears that [cf. *ēcika ōma*]
ēhāha *IPC* oh yes, oh boy

ēkā *IPC* no, not

ēko *PR* that aforementioned one [animate or inanimate proximate singular; cf. *ēwako*]

ēkoni *PrA* that aforementioned one, those aforementioned ones [animate obviative pronoun]

ēkos īsi *IPH* in this way, like this [also: *ēkosi isi*]

ēkosi *IPC* so, thus, in that way; so then; that's it, that's all

ēkospīhk *IPC* at that time

ēkot ānima *IPH* it was there [also: *ēkota anima*]

ēkota *IPC* there, at that aforementioned place

ēkotē *IPC* over there

ēkotowa *IPC* that kind [cf. *ēkwatowa*]

ēkw ānima *IPH* then it was, then the time came; now that's it, and that's it [also: *ēkwa anima*]

ēkwa *IPC* and; then; now

ēkwa mīna *IPH* and also

ēkwatowa *IPC* that kind [cf. *ēkotowa*]

ēkwān ēsa *IPH* and then apparently [cf. *ēkwāni IPC*, *ēsa IPC*]

ēkwāni *IPC* and then; it was then

ēkwāni āsay *IPH* that's it already

ēnc *IPC* well! geez! [exclamation of surprise or disgust; also: *nc*]

ēsa *IPC* evidently, apparently [evidential; reference to time past; information received from others, often traditional knowledge]

ētikwē *IPC* I guess, apparently, presumably; I wonder

ēwako *PR* that aforementioned one [animate or inanimate proximate singular; cf. *ēko*]

ēwakoni *PrI* those ones, those aforementioned ones [inanimate plural pronoun; cf. wC: *iyakoni*]

ēwakoýikohk *IPC* that much, to that extent

ēwakw ānima *IPH* that's the one [also: *ēwako anima*]

ēwakw ēci awa *IPH* so this is who, so that's the one [cf. *ēcika IPC*]

ēy *IPC* hey! my goodness

hā *IPC* hah! there! [exclamation]

hāāy *IPC* whoa! oh my!
hām *IPC* all right, okay!
hāw *IPC* well, okay, all right; see here; let's go [cf. *āw*]
icikātī- *VII* be so called, be told thus [wC; e.g. *kā-kī-icikātīki* "that they were called"; cf. pC: *icikātē-*]
ihtasi- *VAI* be so numbered, be in such a number [commonly plural, e.g. *ihtasiwak* "they are in such a number"]
ikos īsi *IPH* in that way [wC: cf. *ēkos īsi*]
ikosi *IPC* so, thus, in that way; so then; that's it, that's all [wC; alternates with *īkosi*; cf. *ēkosi*]
ikota *IPC* there [wC; alternates with *īkota*; cf. *ēkota*]
ikotī *IPC* over there [wC; alternates with *īkotī*, cf. *ēkotē*]
ikwa *IPC* and; then [wC; alternates with *īkwa*; cf. *ēkwa*]
ikwa mīna *IPH* and also [wC; cf. *ēkwa mīna*]
iňa *IPC* [emphatic particle; sC; cf. *wīňa*; pC: *wiýa*; wC: *wītha*]
*Indian*iwi- *VAI* be an Indian [loanword integrated into Cree structure; e.g. *namōtha niwī*-Indian*iwin* "I'm not going to be an Indian"]
iňikohk *IPC* so much, to such a degree, to such an extent [sC; cf. *iýikohk*]
iňiniw- *NA* person, human being; Indian person [sC; e.g. *iňiniwa* "people [obviative]"; cf. pC: *iýiniw-*]
isi *IPC* thus, in such a way; in such a direction
isi- *IPV* thus, so, in such a way; in such a direction [e.g. *kī-ay-is-ātaýōhkāniwiw* "sacred stories were told so"; e.g. *ē-kī-isi-pēhtamān* "(as) I had thus heard"; e.g. *tānisi ē-kī-isi-atoskēcik* "how their work was going"; e.g. wC: *kā-kī-isi-mītawīyāhk* "how we played"; e.g. wC: *kā-kī-pī-is-ōhpikiyāhk* "how we came to grow up"]
isi-ayāw- *VTA* have s.o. so, have s.o. in such a position [e.g. *kī-isi-ayāwēwak* "they had him so"]
isimākwan- *VII* smell so, smell thus, have such a smell [e.g. *ē-isimākwahk* "(as) it smells so"]
isinākosi- *VAI* appear so, have such an appearance [e.g. *nāpēsis ē-isinākosit* "he looks like a little boy"]
isiniskē- *VAI* move one's hand so, make such a gesture with one's hand [e.g. *ē-isiniskēt* "(as) she gestures"]

isithihkāt- *VTI* call s.t. thus; name s.t. thus [wC; e.g. *nikī-isithihkātīnān* "I called them …"; cf. pC: *isiýihkāt-*]

isithihkātī- *VII* be called thus, be so named [wC; e.g. *kī-isithihkātīw* "it was called …"; cf. pC: *isiýihkātē-*]

isiwēpin- *VTA* throw s.o. thus, throw s.o. there [e.g. *nitisiwēpinâw* "I throw it so"]

isiýihkāso- *VAI* be called so, be so named [e.g. *tānis ōma ē-isiýihkāsoyēk* "how is it that you are called; what is your name"]

isiýihkātiso- *VAI* call oneself so, give oneself such a name [e.g. *ta-kī-isiýihkātisoyēk* "you should call yourselves so"]

isīhtā- *VAIt* make s.t. thus, prepare s.t. thus, manufacture s.t. thus [e.g. *ay-isīhtāw* "he makes them thus"]

isko *IPC* up to, until

iskonikan- *NI* reserve, reserve land [locative: *iskonikanihk* "on the reserve"]

iskwāhtēm- *NI* door [e.g. locative: *iskwāhtēmihk* "on the door, at the door"]

iskwēw- *NA* woman [e.g. *iskwēwak* "women"]

iskwīyānihk *IPC* last, at the end [wC; cf. *iskwēyānihk*]

ispahtā- *VAI* run there; run thus [e.g. *ispahtāw* "he runs (there)"]

ispańi- *VII* happen, occur so [sC; e.g. *kī-ati-ay-ispańińiw* "it came to pass"; cf. pC: *ispaýi-*]

ispaýi- *VII* happen so, occur thus; travel there [e.g. *ē-kī-ispaýik* "(as) it happened"]

ispī *IPC* when; at the time [cf. *ispīhk*]

ispīhcā- *VII* be such a size, reach so far in extent [e.g. *ē-ispīhcāk* "as far as it extends"]

ispīhk *IPC* when, at the time [cf. *ispī*]

it- *VTA* say so to s.o., tell s.o. thus; call s.o. so [e.g. *itēw* "he says to her"; e.g. *nitik* "he says to me", also: *nititik*; e.g. *kā-kī-itikot* "when he said to her"; e.g. wC: *ī-itikawiyāhk* "(as) we are told"; e.g. *kā-kī-itiht* "(he) who was called …"; e.g. *nikī-itikawin* "I was told"; e.g. *nitikawinān* "we are told so; it is said of us"; *kā-itāt* "which she says to her; when he said so to her"; *nikī-itik* "he told me"] ita *IPC* there; where

itahkamikisi- *VAI* be occupied with, be busy with, do so [e.g. *kā-itahkamikisit* "what he is doing"; *ē-kī-pē-itahkamikisit* "(that) he has come to do"; e.g. *kā-kī-pē-ay-itahkamikisicik* "what they had been up to"]

itakiso- *VAI* be counted so, be considered so; be worth so much, be of such a value [e.g. wC: *nikī-nōhtī-itakison* "I wanted to be considered"; e.g. wC: *ī-itakisoyan* "(as) you value yourself so"]

itācimo- *VAI* tell news thus, tell a story so [e.g. *ē-itācimoyāhk* "(as) we told about it"]

itē *IPC* there, thereabouts, where

itēýiht- *VTI* think, think about s.t., think so about s.t. [e.g. *ē-kī-ay-itēýihtamān* "(as) I was thinking"]

itēyihti- *VAI* be away for a length of time [e.g. *kinwēsīs itēyihtiw* "he was away for a little while"]

itēýim- *VTA* think so of s.o. [e.g. *nitēýimāw* "I think so of her"; also: *nititēýimāw*]

itīthiht- *VTI* think so, think about s.t. so [wC; e.g. *ī-itīthihtaman* "(as) you think …"; cf. pC: *itēýiht-*]

itīthimiso- *VTA* think so of oneself [wC; e.g. *ta-kī-itīthimisoyan* "you should think … of yourself"; cf. pC: *itēýimiso-*]

itohtah- *VTA* take s.o. there [e.g. *itohtahēwak* "they take him there"; *itohtahihk* "(all of you), take him there!"]

itohtē- *VAI* go, go there [e.g. *kī-pē-itohtēwak* "they came"; e.g. *kā-kī-wī-itohtēcik* "(where) they were going to go"]

itohtī- *VAI* go, go there [wC; e.g. *kā-kī-itohtīyān* "when I went (there)"; cf. *itohtē-*]

itōt - *VTI* do so, do s.t. thus [e.g. *kā-kī-isi-itōtamāhk* "that we had been doing"]

itōtaw- *VTA* do ill to s.o.; have a bad effect on s.o. [e.g. *kika-māýi-tōtākon* "it will do you ill"]

itwē- *VAI* say so, say thus [e.g. *itwēw* "s/he says it"; e.g. *ē-itwēcik* "(as) they say"; e.g. *ē-itwēhk* "(as) it is said"; e.g. *k-ētwēt* "which s/he says"; e.g. *nitay-itwān* "I say"]

itwēńit- *VTI* think so, think so about s.t. [sC; e.g. *nititwēńitēn* "I think so"; cf. pC: *itēýiht-*]

itwī- *VAI* say so [wC; e.g. *itwīw* "he says"; e.g. *nikī-itwān* "I said"; cf. *itwē-*]

iyakoni *PrI* those ones [wC; inanimate plural pronoun; cf. *ēwakoni*]

iyakw ānima *PrI* that one, that's the one [wC; alternates with *iyako anima*; cf. *ēwakw ānima, ēwako anima*]

iýinito *IPN* ordinary, regular, typical; real [e.g. *iýinito-mostosak* "cows"]

iýinito-mostos- *NA* cow; buffalo [e.g. *iýinito-mostosak* "cows"]

ī- *IPV* that, as [wC; marker of conjunct mode; cf. *ē-*]

īhī *IPC* oh my, geez

īkospī *IPC* at that time [wC; alternates with *ikospī*; cf. *ēkospī*]

īkota *IPC* there [wC; alternates with *ikota*; cf. *ēkota*]

īkwa *IPC* and; then [wC; alternates with *ikwa*; cf. *ēkwa*]

īsa *IPC* evidently, apparently [wC; evidential; reference to time past; information received from others, often traditional knowledge; cf. *ēsa*]

ka- *IPV* ongoing, continuative [light reduplication of /k/-initial stems; e.g. *kiwī-ka-kociskāsināwāw* "you (all) are going to race against me"]

ka- *IPV* to, in order to [marker of conjunct; future infinitival; e.g. *ka-sīpēkistikwānēnāt* "for her to wash his hair"; e.g. *ka-miýo-tēpihtiniýik* "for it [obviative] to fit in well"; cf. *ta-*]

ka- *IPV* will [future tense; often restricted to first and second person independent mode reference; e.g. *nika-ācimon* "I will tell a story"; e.g. *ka-kīwēhtahānaw* "we will take it home"; e.g. *k-ōsīhtamātin* "I will make it for you"; e.g. *kika-māýi-tōtākon* "it will do you ill"; e.g. sC: *ka-mīńāw* "you will give (her) to him"]

kahkińaw *IPC* all, all of [sC; cf. pC: *kahkiýaw*]

kahkiýaw *IPC* all, all of [cf. sC: *kahkińaw*]

kahkiýaw kīkway *IPH* everything, all things [cf. *kīkway- PR*]

kakwē- *IPV* try to [e.g. *ē-kakwē-isi-pimācihocik* "(as) they try to make a living so"; e.g. *kā-kī-kakwē-sīpēkistikwānēnisot* "when he tried to wash his own hair"]

kakwēcim- *VTA* ask s.o.; ask it of s.o. [e.g. *kā-kakwēcimāt* "when she asks him"] kanawāpaht- *VTI* watch s.t., view s.t. [e.g. wC: *nikī-kanawāpahtīnān* "we watched it"; e.g. wC: *ī-kī-nitawi-kanawāpahtamāhk* "(as) we went to watch it"]

kanawāpam- *VTA* watch s.o., look at s.o. [e.g. *kanawāpamēwak* "they look at him"; e.g. *ta-kanawāpamak* "for me to watch him"]

kanawīthim- *VTA* take care of s.o., look after s.o. [wC; e.g. *kā-kī-kanawīthimikoyāhk* "he (who) looked after us"; cf. pC: *kanawēýim-*]

kapī *IPC* all the time, all along [wC; cf. *kapē*]

kaskihtā- *VAI* be able to, have the ability to do s.t. [e.g. *ē-kaskihtāt* "(as) he is able to do it"]

kaskikwāt- *VTA* sew s.o. [as an animate piece of clothing; e.g. *ē-kaskikwātāt* "(as) she sews them"]

kawisimo- *VAI* go to bed; get ready for sleep [e.g. *kī-kawisimowak* "they went to bed"]

kawisimonah- *VTA* put s.o. to bed; lay s.o. to rest [e.g. *kī-kawisimonahāw* "he was laid to rest"]

kayās *IPC* long ago

kayāsēs *IPC* a while ago, quite some time ago

kā- *IPV* that, which; where, when [relative clause marker; conjunct mode marker; e.g. *itē kā-wīkit* "where s/he lives"; *kā-takohtēcik* "when they arrived"; e.g. *kā-miskawāyēk* "which you have found"; e.g. *kā-itāt* "when he said so to her"; e.g. *kā-kāh-kimotamawit* "which he keeps stealing from me"; e.g. *kā-kī-awāsisīwiyān* "when I was a child"; e.g. *kā-nōhtēhkatēt* "he who is hungry"]

kāh- *IPV* repeatedly, iteratively; augmentative [heavy reduplication of /k/-initial stems; e.g. *kāh-kitāpamēwak* "they examined it all over; they really looked it over"; e.g. *nikāh-kimotamāk* "he keeps stealing from me"; e.g. *kā-kāh-kēýakisit* "that he kept having an itch"; e.g. wC: *ī-kī-nitawi-kāh-kiskinwahamākosiyāhk* "(as) we were attending school"]

kāh- *IPV* would, could [e.g. *kāh-ati-patinahk* "that she would have dropped it"]

kāhcitin- *VTA* catch s.o. [e.g. *kā-kāhcitinācik* "when they caught it"]

kāhkēwakos- *NI* small piece of dried meat [diminutive; cf. *kāhkēwakw-*]

kāhkēwakw- *NI* dried meat [e.g. *kāhkēwak* "dried meat"]
kāsīhkwē- *VAI* wash one's own face [e.g. *ē-kīsi-kāsīhkwēt* "(as) he finishes washing his face"]
kāsōpańiho- *VAI* throw oneself into hiding [sC; e.g. *kāsōpańihow* "he throws himself into hiding"; cf. pC: *kāsōpaýiho-*]
kāwińa *IPC* don't [sC; negative imperative; cf. pC: kāwiýa]
kē- *IPV* [future tense, conjunct mode form; e.g. *kē-takopahtāt* "he will arrive running"; e.g. *kē-wāpahk* "when dawn arrives; in the morning"]
kē- *IPV* would [hypothetical mood, conjunct mode form; e.g. kē-mīcit "he would eat"]
kēhtē-ayiwi- *VAI* be old, be an elder [e.g. *ē-kēhtē-ayiwicik* "(as) they are old"]
kēkāc *IPC* almost, nearly
kēkisēpā- *VII* be morning [sC; e.g. *ē-kēkisēpāńik* "(as) it is morning"; cf. *kīkisēpā IPC*]
kēkwāń- *PR* something, thing [sC; often unmarked for number; cf. pC and wC: *kīkway-*]
kētahtawē *IPC* suddenly, all of a sudden; at one time; eventually
kētahtawēn *IPC* suddenly, all of a sudden; at one time [sC; cf. *kētahtawē*]
kēýakiciskē- *VAI* have an itchy butt [cf. *okēýakiciskēsīsak* "Little Butt Itchers"]
kēýakiciskēhiwē- *VAI* make people's butts itchy, give people itchy butts [cf. *okēýakiciskēhiwēsīsak* "Little Butt-Itch-Makers"]
kēýakisi- *VAI* be itchy, have an itch [e.g. *kika-misi-kēýakisin* "you will be very itchy"]
kēyāpic *IPC* still, more, further
kihci- *IPV* greatly, a great deal [e.g. *ē-kihci-wīcihihcik* "(as) they receive welfare"]
kihci-wīcih- *VTA* help s.o. a great deal; provide welfare to s.o. [commonly in unspecified actor form; e.g. *ē-kihci-wīcihihcik* "(as) they receive welfare"; cf. *kihci- IPV*, *wīcih- VTA*]
kiki *IPC* with; in addition to

kimotamaw- *VTA* steal (it/him) from s.o. [e.g. *kī-kāh-kimotamāk* "he kept being stolen from by (this other)"; e.g. *kā-kāh-kimotamawit* "he who kept stealing from me"]

kinwāpēkan- *VII* be long (as a stick) [e.g. *ē-kinwāpēkaniyik* "(as) it [obviative] is long"]

kinwēs *IPC* a long while, for a long time

kinwēsīs *IPC* a while, quite a while

kipihtin- *VII* stop, be stopped, come to an end [e.g. *ē-kipihtik* "(as) it stops, (as) it comes to an end"]

kisēyiniw- *NA* old man [e.g. *kisēyiniwak* "old men"; e.g. *misi-kisēyiniw* "big old man"]

kisiwāsi- *VAI* be angry, be mad [e.g. *kā-kisiwāsit* "that she was angry"]

kisīpahtā- *VAI* run fast, run quickly [e.g. *nimāwaci-kisīpahtān* "I run fastest of all"]

kiskēyiht- *VTI* know, know s.t. [e.g. *nikiskēyihtēn* "I know it"; e.g. *kiskēyihtam* "he knows it"; e.g. *kī-kiskēyihtamwak* "they knew it"]

kiskēyim- *VTA* know s.o. [e.g. *kikiskēyimāw cī?* "do you know him?"]

kiskinwahamākosi- *VAI* learn, attend school [e.g. *ī-nitawi-kiskinwahamākosiyāhk* "(as) we go to attend school"]

kiskinwahamātowikamikw- *NI* school [e.g. locative *kiskinwahamātowikamikohk* "at the school"]

kiskisi- *VAI* remember [e.g. *nikiskisinān* "we remember"]

kispakwastā- *VAIt* put s.t. on thickly, set s.t. thick [e.g. *kā-misi-kispakwastāt* "that which he put on very thickly"]

kistapinānihk *INM* Prince Albert, SK [locative; e.g. *kistapi- VAI* "sit well, be in a good position, be well off"]

kitamw- *VTA* eat s.o. all up, devour s.o. [e.g. *kitamwēw* "he devoured it"; *ē-kī-kitamwāt* "(as) he had eaten it all"]

kitāpam- *VTA* look at s.o. [e.g. *kāh-kitāpamēwak* "they examined it all over; they really looked it over"]

kitimākisi- *VAI* be pitiful, desolate, destitute; be poor [e.g. *kitimākisiw* "he is pitiable"; e.g. *kī-kitimākisiwak* "they were pitiful, desolate"; e.g. *kikitimākisin* "you are pitiful"]

kiyokaw- *VTA* visit s.o. [e.g. *ē-kī-kiyokawakik* "(as) I was visiting them"]

kiyokāto- *VAI* visit one another [e.g. *kī-papā-kiyokātowak* "they went about visiting one another"; e.g. *kā-kiyokātoyāhk* "when we visit one another"]

kī- *IPV* [past tense; e.g. *kī-pimohtēskiw* "he always wandered about"; e.g. *kī-nisitawinawēwak* "they recognized it"; e.g. *ē-kī-ācimocik* "as they told stories"; e.g. *ē-kī-ispaýik* "(as) it happened"; e.g. sC: *ē-kī-nipahāńit* "(as) they killed it"; e.g. *kā-kī-awāsisīwiyān* "when I was a child"]

kīkisēpā *IPC* in the morning [cf. sC: *kēkisēpā- VII*]

kīkway- *NA* thing [e.g. *kīkwaya* "the thing [obviative]"; cf. *kīkway- PR*]

kīkway *NI* thing [e.g. *kīkwaya* "things"; sometimes unmarked for singular and plural interchangeably; cf. *kīkway- PR*; cf. sC: *kēkwān*]

kīkway *PR* something [animate or inanimate singular indefinite pronoun]

kīkwāy- *PR* what [animate proximate or inanimate singular interrogative pronoun]

kīkwāya *PrA* what [animate obviative interrogative pronoun; cf. *kīkwāy-*]

kīkwāya *PrI* what [inanimate proximate or obviative plural pronoun; e.g. *kīkwāya* "what [obviative]"]

kīsi- *IPV* finish, complete [e.g. *kī-kīsi-sīpēkistikwānēw* "he finished washing his own hair"; e.g. *ē-kīsi-kāsīhkwēt* "(as) he finishes washing his face"]

kīsikā- *VII* be day, be daylight [e.g. *kā-kīsikāk* "when it was day; that day"]

kīsikāw- *NI* day [cf. *kīsikā- VII*]

kīsōsi- *VAI* be warm [e.g. *nika-kīsōsin* "I will be warm"]

kīspo- *VAI* be full (from eating), be fully fed [e.g. *nikīspon* "I am full"; e.g. *ē-kīspot* "(as) he is full"]

kītahtawī *IPC* suddenly, all of a sudden; at one time; eventually [wC; cf. *kētahtawē*] kītha *PR* you, yours [wC; second person singular personal pronoun; cf. pC: *kiýa*, sC: *kińa*]

kītim *NDA* your (cross-) cousin (of opposite gender); your sister-in-law (in relation to a male); your brother-in-law (in relation to a female) [second person singular possessive form; cf. *-ītimw-*]

kīwē- *VAI* go home [e.g. *pē-āsē-kīwēw* "he comes back homewards"; e.g. *kā-kī-āpani-kīwēt* "when he turned back homewards"]

kīwēhtah- *VTA* take s.o. home, carry s.o. home [e.g. *kā-kīwēhtahānaw* "we will take it home"]

kīwēpahtā- *VAI* run home [e.g. *pē-āsē-kīwēpahtāw* "he comes running back homewards"]

kīwētinohk *IPC* north, in the north [locative; cf. *kīwētin(w)- NI* "north wind; the north"]

kociskāt- *VTA* race against s.o.; run a race against s.o. [e.g. *kiwī-ka-kociskāsināwāw* "you (all) are going to race against me"]

kohkōsiwiyin- *NA* bacon

konita *IPC* for nothing, merely, just

kost- *VTI* be afraid of s.t. [e.g. *ē-kī-kostahk* "(that) he was afraid of it"]

kotak *PR* other, another [animate or inanimate indefinite singular pronoun]

kwayask *IPC* right, correct; correctly, properly

kwēyask *IPC* right, correct; correctly, properly [also: *kwayask*]

ma kīkway *IPH* nothing; there was nothing

ma- *IPV* ongoing, continuative [light reduplication of /m/-initial stems; e.g. *ē-ma-minihkwēcik* "(as) they are drinking"; *ē-ma-mīcisosicik* "(as) they are snacking"; e.g. sC: *ma-mēkwāpańīstawēw* "he met up with them"]

macēńim- *VTA* think ill of s.o., be mistrustful of s.o. [sC: e.g. *macēńimēwak* "they are mistrustful of him"; cf. pC: *macēýim-*]

mahihkan- *NA* wolf [e.g. *mahihkana* "wolves [obviative]"]

mahti *IPC* let's see (it); please

mamihcimo- *VAI* boast, brag; be boastful [e.g. *māci-mamihcimow* "he starts to boast"]

manis- *VTI* cut s.t. off [e.g. *manisētān* "let's cut it off"]
maskihkīwiýiniw- *NA* medicine man, herbalist; doctor
matwē- *IPV* visibly; audibly, loudly; noticeably [e.g. *matwē-ay-apiw* "he was sitting in view"; *ē-matwē-tēpwātāt* "he is calling to her loudly"; *matwē-itwēw* "s/he says so as to be heard"]
matwēhtahikē- *VAI* make a knocking sound, knock audibly [e.g. *kā-nitawi-matwēhtahikēt* "when she went to knock"]
mawīhkāt- *VTA* cry for s.o.; cry from missing s.o. [e.g. wC: *kī-māh-mawīhkātīwak* "they were crying from missing them"]
māci- *IPV* start to, begin to [e.g. *māci-mamihcimow* "he starts to boast"; e.g. *ē-māci-nōtinitocik* "(as) they start fighting one another"]
mācihtā- *VAIt* start s.t., begin work on s.t. [e.g. *kā-kī-mācihtāyāhk* "when we started …"]
mācīwiýiniw- *NA* hunter [e.g. *mācīwiýiniwak* "hunters"]
māh- *IPV* repeatedly, iteratively; augmentative [heavy reduplication of /m/-initial stems; e.g. wC: *kī-māh-mawīhkātīwak* "they were crying from missing them"; e.g. *nikī-māh-mōcikihtānān* "we really had fun"; e.g. *ē-māh-mōskopitāt* "(as) he kept making it cry out by pulling"; e.g. *ē-māh-mihkosiýit* "(as) they are really red"]
māka *IPC* but; and
māmaskāt- *VTI* be amazed by s.t., be surprised by s.t. [e.g. *kī-māmaskātamwak* "they were amazed by it"]
māna *IPC* usually, habitually, generally, always; used to
māńēńim- *VTA* think ill of s.o.; challenge s.o. [sC; e.g. *māńēńimēw* "he challenges them"; cf. pC: *māýēýim-*]
mātāh- *VTA* track s.o., follow s.o.'s tracks [e.g. *ati-mātāhēw* "he starts following her tracks"]
mātāhiso- *VAI* track oneself, follow one's own tracks [e.g. *kā-mātāhisot* "(that) he was tracking himself"]
mātinawi-kīsikā- *VII* be Saturday [wC; e.g. *kā-mātinawi-kīsikāk* "on Saturdays; when it was Saturday"]
māto- *VAI* cry, wail [e.g. *misi-mātoýiwa* "it [obviative] really wailed"]
māwaci- *IPV* most, foremost, utmost [e.g. *nimāwaci-kisīpahtān* "I run fastest of all"]

māwasakonito- *VAI* gather one another together [e.g. wC: *ī-kī-māwasakonitoyāhk* "(as) we gathered together (into groups)"]
māýi- *IPV* ill, badly [e.g. *kika-māýi-tōtākon* "it will do you ill"]
māýi-tōtaw- *VTA* do ill to s.o.; have a bad effect on s.o. [e.g. *kika-māýi-tōtākon* "it will do you ill"]
māýihkāso- *VAI* have a bad name, have an ugly name, be ill-named [e.g. *kimāýihkāsonāwāw* "you have a bad name"]
mēkwāc *IPC* while, meanwhile, currently
mēkwāpańīstaw- *VTA* meet up with s.o.; be somewhere simultaneously with s.o. [sC; e.g. *ma-mēkwāpańīstawēw* "he met up with them"]
mētoni *IPC* really; very; a great deal [cf. *mitoni*]
micihciy- *NDI* hand [unspecified possessor form, e.g. *micihciya* "hands"; cf. *-cihciy- NDI*]
mihkosi- *VAI* be red [e.g. *ē-māh-mihkosiýit* "(as) they are really red"]
minaho- *VAI* catch wild game; hunt game, make a kill [e.g. *kā-isi-minahoyān* "how I caught my game"]
minihkwē- *VAI* drink, drink s.t. [e.g. *ē-ma-minihkwēcik* "(as) they are drinking"]
miscēt *IPC* many, quite a few [cf. *mihcēt*]
miscikos- *NI* stick, small stick [diminutive; cf. *mistikw-*]
misi- *IPN* big, large; very, greatly [e.g. *misi-mistiýiniw* "a very large individual"]
misi- *IPV* big, large; a lot, much, greatly; very, really [e.g. *ē-misi-nōcihāt* "(as) he beat it severely, (as) he really meaned on it"; *misi-mātoýiwa* "it [obviative] really wailed"; e.g. *kā-misi-kispakwastāt* "that which he put on very thickly"; e.g. *misi-mowēw* "s/he eats a great deal"]
misi-kisēýiniw- *NA* big old man
misikiti- *VAI* be big [e.g. *kī-misikitiw* "it was big"]
misit- *NDI* foot [unspecified possessor form; e.g. *misita* "feet"; cf. *-sit- NDI*]
misk- *VTI* find s.t. [e.g. *kā-miskahk* "that which he found"]
miskaw- *VTA* find s.o. [e.g. *kā-miskawāyēk* "which you have found"]

misoy- *NDI* tail [unspecified possessor form; cf. *-soy- NDI*]
mis-ōkiniy- *NA* large rose-hip [cf. *misi- IPN*, *okiniy- NA*]
mistahi *IPC* a lot, much, greatly
mistahi kīkway *IPH* many things [cf. *mistahi IPC*, *kīkway- NI, PR*]
mistastis- *NA* large mitt, big mitt [e.g. *mistastisa* "big mitts [obviative]"]
mistikw- *NA* tree [e.g. locative: *mistikohk* "on the tree"]
mistiýiniw- *NA* big man, big individual, big Indian person
mithwīthiht- *VTI* like s.t.; be happy [wC; e.g. *nimithwīthihtīn* "I like it"; cf. pC: *miýwēýiht-*]
miton ōti *IPC* very much so; really [also: *mitoni oti*]
mitoni *IPC* really; very [cf. *mētoni*]
miý- *VTA* give (s.t./s.o.) to s.o., give s.o. s.t. [e.g. *nimiýāw* "I give it to her"; *kā-miýikawiyahk* "which we were given"; cf. sC: *miń-*]
miyaw- *NDI* body [unspecified possessor form; cf. *-iyaw-*]
miýāht- *VTI* smell s.t., sniff s.t. [e.g. *ē-miýāhtahk* "(as) she smells it"]
miýo- *IPV* well; good [e.g. *kā-miýo-tēpihtiniýik* "which will fit in well"]
miýo-ācimowin- *NI* good story, good news
mīci- *VAIt* eat s.t. [e.g. *mīciw* "he eats it", e.g. *ka-mīcicik* "for them to eat"; *kā-mīciyān* "which I am eating"; rhetorically extended: *mīīīciw*]
mīciso- *VAI* eat [e.g. *kā-misi-mīcisoyan* "that you are eating a great deal"; e.g. *ē-pōni-mīcisocik* "(as) they stopped eating"]
mīcisosi- *VAI* eat a little; snack; nibble at food [diminutive; e.g. *ē-mā-mīcisosicik* "(as) they are eating"; cf. *mīciso- VAI* "eat"]
mīcisowikamikw- *NI* café, restaurant [e.g. locative: *mīcisowikamikohk* "at the restaurant"]
mīhýawēkasākēsi- *VAI* have a hairy little coat, have a bit of a shaggy coat [diminutive; e.g. *ē-mīhýawēkasākēsit* "(as) he has a hairy little coat", cf. *mīhýawēkasākē-*]
mīń- *VTA* give (s.t./s.o.) to s.o; give s.o. s.t. [sC; e.g. *ka-mīńaw* "you will give (her) to him"; cf. pC: *miý-*]

mīna *IPC* and, also
mītawī- *VAI* play, play games [wC; e.g. *ī-nitawi-mītawīyāhk* "(as) we go to play"; e.g. *nikī-mītawānān* "we played"; cf. pC and sC: *mētawē-*]
mosci- *IPV* merely, just; without instrumentality [e.g. *mosci-kanawāpamēw* "he just watches them"]
mosētiyēhkwāmi- *VAI* sleep with a bare bum, sleep with an exposed bottom [e.g. *kā-mosētiyēhkwāmit* "he who slept with a bare bum"]
mostos- *NA* cow [e.g. *iýinito-mostosak* "cows"]
mow- *VTA* eat s.o. [e.g. *misi-mowēw* "s/he eats a great deal of it [animate]"; e.g. *ē-kī-mowāýit* "(as) he was eating (the others)"]
mōcikihtā- *VAIt* have fun; have fun with s.t., enjoy s.t. [e.g. *nikī-mōcikihtānān* "we had fun"; *nikī-māh-mōcikihtānān* "we really had fun"]
mōńa *IPC* no, not [sC; cf. pC: *mōýa*; wC: *mōtha*]
mōniyāw- *NA* whiteman, non-First Nations Canadian [e.g. *mōniyāwak* "whitemen"]
mōsihtā- *VAIt* feel s.t., sense s.t. [e.g. *kā-mōsihtāt* "that which he felt"]
mōskopit- *VTA* make s.o. cry by pulling, yank the tears out of s.o. [e.g. *ē-māh-mōskopitāt* "(as) he kept making it cry out by pulling"]
mōsw- *NA* moose [e.g. singular or obviative: *mōswa* "moose"]
mōtha *IPC* no, not [wC; cf. *namōtha*; pC: *mōýa*; sC: *mōńa*]
mōý *IPC* no, not [cf. *mōýa, namōýa*]
mōýa *IPC* no, not [cf. *mōý*, *namōýa*; sC: *mōńa*; wC: *mōtha*]
mwāc *IPC* no, not, not at all, no way
mwēhci *IPC* right then, just then, immediately; exactly [cf. *mwēsci*]
mwēsci *IPC* right then, just then, immediately; exactly [cf. *mwēhci*]
nahań- *VTA* bury s.o., inter s.o., lay s.o. to rest [sC; e.g. *kā-kī-isi-nahańācik* "that's how they laid them to rest"; cf. *nahah-*]
nahastā- *VAIt* put s.t. away, store s.t. away [e.g. *kā-nahastāt* "which she put away"]

nakat- *VTA* leave s.o., leave s.o. behind, abandon s.o. [e.g. *nakatēw* "s/he left him/her"; e.g. *kā-kī-nakatiht* "she who had been left"]

nakiskaw- *VTA* meet s.o. [e.g. *nipē-nakiskawāw* "I come to meet (him)"]

nama kīkway *IPH* nothing, not a thing [cf. *ma kīkway*]

namōtha *IPC* no, not [wC; cf. *mōtha*; pC: *namōýa*]

namōýa *IPC* no, not [cf. *mōý*, *mōýa*; *namōýa wīhkāc IPH*; wC: *namōtha*]

namōýa ahpō *IPH* not even

namōýa nānitaw *IPH* nothing, not anything; fine, nothing wrong [often as complement of relative root verb; e.g. *namōýa nānitaw ay-itwēw* "she didn't say a thing"]

namōýa wīhkāc *IPH* never [cf. *namōýa IPC, wīhkāc IPC*]

nawac *IPC* more, moreso

nawac piko *IPH* sort of, kind of, more or less, approximately

nawaciko *IPC* more or less, kind of, sort of [cf. *nawac piko IPH*]

nawacī- *VAI* roast, make a roast [e.g. *ē-nāh-nawacīýit* "that s/he would keep roasting"]

nayēstaw *IPC* only, exclusively; it is only that

nā *IPC* [sC; interrogative particle; follows an element in initial, focus position to indicate a yes-no question; cf. *cī*]

nāh- *IPV* repeatedly, iteratively; augmentative [heavy reduplication of /n/-initial stems; e.g. *ē-nāh-nawacīýit* "that s/he would keep roasting"]

nānitaw *IPC* about, around [cf. *nānitaw isi IPH, namōýa nānitaw IPH*]

nānitaw isi *IPH* in case, in the event (that) [e.g. *nānitaw isi nipiyāni* "in case I die"]

nāpēsis- *NA* boy, little boy

nāpēw- *NA* man

nāpēwi- *VAI* be a man, be male; be in the form of a man [e.g. *kī-nāpēwiw* "he was a man"]

nāpīw- *NA* man [wC; cf. *nāpēw*]

nāsiwē- *VAI* go for supplies [e.g. *nāsiwēw* "he goes for supplies"; e.g. *nikī-nāsiwān* "I went for supplies"] nātakwē- *VAI* check one's own snares [e.g. *kī-nātakwēwak* "they checked their snares]

nātawihiwē- *VAI* heal people, doctor people [e.g. *ē-nātawihiwēt* "(as) he heals people"]

nēhiýaw- *IPN* Cree, Cree object; pertaining to Cree culture or Cree things

nēhiýaw- *NA* Cree man, Cree person [cf. wC: *nīhithaw-*]

nēhiýawitotamowin- *NI* Cree speech

nētē *IPC* over there, over yonder

nicawāsimis- *NDA* my child [first person singular possessive form; e.g. *nicawāsimisinānak* "our children"; cf. *-cawāsimis-*]

nicāhkos- *NDA* [female speaker only:] my female cross-cousin; my sister-in-law [first person singular possessive form; cf. *-cāhkos-* "(female cross-) cousin; my sister-in-law"]

nicīmin *NDA* my younger brother; my younger sibling [*sic*; vocative; cf. *-sīm-*, *-sīmis-*; also *-cīmic-*]

nihtā- *IPV* be adept at, be good at, be skilled at; be known for skill at [e.g. *ē-nihtā-pāhpihikawiyān* "(as) people enjoy laughing at me"]

nikamo- *VAI* sing [e.g. *nāh-nikamowak* "they keep singing"]

nikāwiy- *NDA* my mother [first person singular possessive form; e.g. *nikāwiya* "my [obviative] mother"; cf. *-kāwiy-*]

nimikiy- *NDI* my scab [first person singular possessive form; cf. *-mikiy- NDI, omikiy- NI*]

nipah- *VTA* kill s.o. [e.g. *ē-kakwē-nipahācik* "(as) they try to kill them"; e.g. *kā-nipahikot* "that which killed him"; e.g. sC: *ē-kī-nipahāńit* "(as) they [obviative] killed it"]

nipahi- *IPV* very, greatly, drastically, killingly, to the death [e.g. *kēkāc ē-nipahi-pāhpiyāhk* "(as) we nearly died laughing"]

nipi- *VAI* die, be dead [e.g. *nipiyāni* "if/when I die"; *ē-nipit* "(as) he is dead"]

nipiy- *NI* water

nisitawin- *VTI* recognize s.t. [e.g. *kā-ati-nisitawinahk* "when he starts to recognize it"] nisitawinaw- *VTA* recognize s.o. [e.g. *nisitawinawēw* "she recognizes him"; e.g. *kī-nisitawinawēwak* "they recognized it"]

nisīm- *NDA* my younger sibling, my little brother, my little sister [first person singular possessive form; e.g. vocative: *nisīmitik* "my younger siblings"; cf. *-sīm-*]

nistam *IPC* first; at first; before anything else

nistēsē *NDA* my older brother! [vocative; cf. *-stēs-*]

nistwāw *IPC* three times, thrice

nitakisa *IPC* yeah, right! not by any chance

nitaw- *IPV* go to, go and [cf. *nitawi-*]

nitawāpahto- *VAI* check up on one another [e.g. *ē-pē-nitawāpahtocik* "(as) they came to check up on one another]

nitawāpēnaw- *VTA* go to check up on s.o. [e.g. *kā-nitawāpēnawāt* "when she went to check up on him"]

nitawēýiht- *VTI* want s.t.; need s.t. [e.g. *ē-nitawēýihtaman* "(as) you want it"]

nitawi- *IPV* go to, go and [e.g. *kī-nitawi-sīpēkistikwānēnisow* "he went to wash his own hair"; e.g. *nikī-nitawi-ayamihcikānān* "we went to attend school"; e.g. wC: *ī-nitawi-kiskinwahamākosiyāhk* "(as) we go to attend school"; cf. *nitaw-*]

nīhithaw- *NA* Cree, Cree man, Cree person [wC; e.g. *nīhithawak* "Crees"; cf. pC: *nēhiýaw-*]

nīkān *IPC* in front, in the lead; in first place, before

nīkāniwēpin- *VTA* throw s.o. in front [e.g. *ninīkaniwēpināw* "I throw it in front"]

nīkihikomāw- *NA* parent [e.g. *ninīkihikomāwak* "my parents"; cf. *-nīkihikw- NDA*]

nīmihitowikamikw- *NI* dance hall [e.g. locative: *nīmihitowikamikohk* "at the dance hall"]

nīńa *PR* I; me; mine [sC; first person singular personal pronoun; cf. pC: *niýa*; wC: *nītha*]

nīsi- *VAI* be two in number, be two together [e.g. sC: *kī-nīsińiwa* "there were two of them [obviative]"]

nīso *IPC* two

nīsowihkāso- *VAI* have two names, be called in two ways [e.g. *nāh-nīsowihkāsonāniwiw* "there are generally two names"]

nīsta *PR* I, too; me, too [first person singular personal pronoun]

nītha *PR* I; me; mine [wC; first person singular personal pronoun; cf. pC: *niýa*; wC: *nīńa*]

nīthanān *PR* we, us, ours [wC; first person plural exclusive personal pronoun; cf. pC: *niýanān*]

nītisān- *NDA* my sibling [first person singular possessive form; e.g. *nītisānak* "my siblings"; cf. *-ītisān-*]

nohcāwīs- *NDA* my uncle, my father's brother [first person singular possessive form; e.g. *nohcāwīsak* "my uncles"; cf. *-ohcāwīs-*]

nohkom *NDA* my grandmother [first person singular possessive form; cf. *-ohkom-*]

nohtāwiy- *NDA* my father [first person singular possessive form; e.g. *nohtāwiya* "my father [obviative]"; cf. *-ohtāwiy-*]

nōcih- *VTA* mean on s.o., beat s.o., mistreat s.o. [e.g. *nōcihēw* "she beats him up"; e.g. *ē-misi-nōcihāt* "(as) he beat it severely, (as) he really meaned on it"]

nōcihtā- *VAIt* work on s.t., struggle with s.t. [e.g. *ē-nōcihtāt* (as) he works on it"]

nōcikwēsiw- *NA* old woman [e.g. *nīso nōcikwēsiwak* "two old women"; cf. *nōtokēsiw-*]

nōhtē- *IPV* want to [e.g. *nōhtē-mīciw* "s/he wants to eat it"]

nōhtēhkatē- *VAI* be hungry [e.g. *nōhtēhkatēw* "s/he is hungry"; e.g. *kā-nōhtēhkatēt* "he who is hungry"]

nōhtī- *IPV* want to [wC; e.g. *nikī-nōhtī-itakison* "I wanted to be considered"; cf. pC: *nōhtē-*]

nōkosi- *VAI* appear, be visible [e.g. sC: *ēkā kā-nōkosińit* "they [obviative] who are not visible"; e.g. wC: *ī-kī-nōkosit* "(as) he appeared"]

nōmakēsīs *IPC* for a while, a little while

nōtinito- *VAI* fight one another [e.g. *ē-māci-nōtinitocik* "(as) they started fighting one another"]

nōtokēsiw- *NA* old woman [cf. *nōcikwēsiw-*]

ohci *IPC* from, from there

ohci- *IPV* from, from there; for, in order to, for the purpose of; with, by means of [e.g. *ē-ohci-asamāwasocik* "in order to feed their children"; e.g. *ka-ohci-sīpēkistikwānēnisoýit* "for him [obviative] to wash his own hair with"]

ohcitaw *IPC* necessarily, obligatorily; must

ohkoma *NDA* his/her grandmother [third person proximate singular animate possessive form; e.g. *nohkom* "my grandmother"; cf. *-ohkom-*]

ohpiki- *VAI* grow, grow up [e.g. wC: *kā-kī-pī-is-ōhpikiyāhk* "how we came to grow up"]

ohpikih- *VTA* raise s.o. [e.g. *kā-kī-is-ōhpikihikawiyāhk* "how we were raised"]

okēýakiciskēhiwēsīs- *NA* Little Butt-Itch-Maker [e.g. *okēýakiciskēhiwēsīsak* "Little Butt-Itch-Makers"; cf. *kēýakiciskēhiwē- VAI*]

okēýakiciskēsīs- *NA* Little Butt Itcher [e.g. *okēýakiciskēsīsak* "Little Butt Itchers"; cf. *kēýakiciskē- VAI*]

okimāhkān- *NA* chief, elected chief

okiniy- *NA* rose-hip [e.g. *okiniya* "rose-hip(s) [obviative]"; e.g. *okiniyak* "rose-hips"]

omikiy- *NI* scab; his/her scab [third person singular possessive and unmarked singular form; cf. *-mikiy- NDI*]

omisi *IPC* like this, in this way

omisimāw- *NA* eldest sister, older sister [e.g. *omisimāwa* "the eldest sister [obviative]"; cf. *-mis- NDA*]

onāpēma *NDA* her husband [third person proximate singular animate possessive form; cf. *-nāpēm-*]

onīkihikwa *NDA* his/her parent(s) [third person proximate singular animate possessive form; e.g. *onīkihikowāwa* "their parents"; cf. *-nīkihikw-*; sometimes *-nēkihikw-* in Plains Cree]

opimipaýihcikēw- *NA* manager, caretaker; chief

osām *IPC* for, because; too much; because of excess

osāpam- *VTA* watch out for s.o., keep a watch for s.o., keep an eye on s.o. [e.g. *ē-osāpamāt* "(as) she keeps an eye on him"]

osāwā- *VII* be orange, be brown [e.g. *ē-osāwāk* "(as) it is orange"] oscikwānis- *NDI* his/her little head [third person proximate singular possessive form; cf. *-scikwānis-*]

osīhtamaw- *VTA* make (it) for s.o. [e.g. *nikī-osīhtamawāw* "I made it for him"]

osīhtā- *VAIt* make s.t., prepare s.t., manufacture s.t. [e.g. *osīhtāw* "he makes it"]

osīkinikēw- *NA* waiter, waitress [e.g. *osīkinikēwa* "waitress [obviative]"]

osīmisa *NDA* his/her younger sibling(s), his/her younger brother(s) or sister(s) [third person proximate singular animate possessive form; cf. *-sīmis-*]

ostēsa *NDA* his/her older brother(s) [third person proximate singular animate possessive form; cf. *-stēs-*]

otākosin- *VII* be evening [e.g. *ē-otākosiniẏik* "(as) it is evening"]

otānisa *NDA* his/her daughter(s) [third person proximate singular animate possessive form; cf. *-tānis-* "daughter"]

oti *IPC* [emphatic particle; emphasizes preceding word]

otiht- *VTA* reach s.o., approach s.o. [e.g. *otihtikoyēko* "when he reaches you"]

otiht- *VTI* reach s.t., approach s.t. [e.g. *otihtam* "he reaches it"; e.g. *kā-at-ōtihtamān* "when I was approaching it"]

otihtin- *VTA* grab s.o., grapple so.; sexually assault s.o. [e.g. *nipē-otihtinik* "she came to grapple me"]

otin- *VTA* take s.o., choose s.o. [e.g. *kā-otināt* "which he took"; e.g. *kā-kī-otinikawiyān* "when I had been chosen"]

otin- *VTI* take s.t. [e.g. *at-ōtinam* "s/he takes it up; e.g. *kā-otinahk* "she who took it; which he took"]

otōpāpāwa *NDA* his/her dad, father [sC; third person proximate singular animate possessive form; e.g. *otōpāpāwāwa* "their dad [obviative]"; cf. *-opāpā-*, *-pāpā-*]

owēscakāsa *NDI* his/her hair [third person proximate singular inanimate possessive form; commonly plural; e.g. *owēscakāsiẏiwa* "his [obviative] hair"; e.g. locative: *owēscakāsihk* "in his hair"; cf. *wēscakās-*; *-ēscakās-*]

ōh- *IPV* from, from there [e.g. *k-ōh-waýawīhk* "from where he voids"; cf. *ohci- IPV*]

ōh- *IPV* have done [e.g. *namōýa wīhkāc ēkotowa nitōh-wāpamāw* "I have never seen that kind"; cf. *ohci- IPV*]

ōhi *PrA* this, this one; these, these ones [animate obviative (singular or plural) pronoun; e.g. *ōhi kīkwaya* "this thing/these things"; cf. sC: *ōho*]

ōhi *PrI* these, these ones [inanimate proximate or obviative plural pronoun]

ōho *PrA* this, this one; these, these ones [sC; animate obviative (singular or plural) pronoun; cf. *ōhi*]

ōki *IPC* it is (these) [focus marker]

ōki *PrA* these, these ones [animate proximate plural pronoun; cf. sC: *ōko*]

ōko *PrA* these, these ones [sC; animate proximate plural pronoun; cf. *ōki*]

ōma *IPC* it is (that) [focus marker; cf. *ōma PrI*]

ōma *PrI* this, this one [inanimate proximate singular pronoun; cf. *ōma IPC*]

ōta *IPC* here, right here

ōtē *IPC* over here, hereabouts

ōtē isi *IPH* this way, hereabouts

ōtī *IPC* over here [wC; cf. *ōtē*]

pa- *IPV* ongoing, continuative [light reduplication of /p/-initial stems; e.g. *ati-wańawī-pa-pakamahwēw* "she pummelled him right outside"; e.g. *ē-pa-pāhpiyāhk* "(as) we were laughing"; e.g. *ē-pa-pimohtēt* "(as) s/he was walking along"]

pahkihtitā- *VAIt* drop s.t. accidentally, let s.t. fall [e.g. *kā-ati-pahkihtitāt* "which he let fall"]

pakamahw- *VTA* hit s.o., strike s.o. [e.g. *nimisi-pakamahwāw* "I gave him a big wallop"; e.g. *ati-wańawī-pa-pakamahwēw* "she pummelled him right outside"; e.g. *ē-pakamahwāt* "(that) she hit him"]

pakonēyā- *VII* have a hole in the middle [e.g. *pakonēyāýiw* "it [obviative] has a hole in the middle"] pamin- *VTA* take care of s.o., look after s.o., tend to s.o. [e.g. *kā-paminācik* "they who are tending to him"]

papā- *IPV* go about, around, all over [e.g. *kī-papā-kiyokātowak* "they went about visiting one another"; cf. *papāmi-*]

papāmi- *IPC* go about, around, all over [e.g. *papāmi-ayāw* "he loitered about, he stayed all over the place"; cf. *papā-*]

papāmohtē- *VAI* wander around, wander about, walk around [e.g. *papāmohtēw* "s/he wanders about"]

pasikōpahtā- *VAI* jump up at a run, stand up running [e.g. *kā-pasikōpahtācik* "when they jumped up at a run"]

paskipaýiho- *VAI* burst forth, break free [e.g. *kā-paskipaýihot* "when he broke free"]

paso- *VAI* smell s.t. [e.g. *kā-pasot* "which she smelled"]

patin- *VTI* drop s.t. [e.g. *kāh-ati-patinahk* "that she would have dropped it"]

pāh- *IPV* repeatedly, iteratively [heavy reduplication of /p/-initial stems; e.g. *pāh-pīmihtawakēnēw* "he kept twisting his ears"]

pāhkohkwēhon- *NI* towel

pāhpi- *VAI* laugh [e.g. *ē-pāhpit* "(as) he is laughing"; e.g. *pāhpināniwan* "there is laughter"; e.g. *ē-pāhpihk* "(as) there is laughter"; e.g. *ē-pa-pāhpiyāhk* "(as) we were laughing"]

pāhpih- *VTA* laugh at s.o. [e.g. *pāhpihēw* "he laughs at them"; e.g. *ē-nihtā-pāhpihikawiyān* "(as) people enjoy laughing at me"]

pāhpipaýi- *VAI* burst out in laughter, laugh suddenly [e.g. *kā-misi-pāhpipaýit* "she who burst out laughing"]

pāhpisi- *VAI* chuckle, laugh a little [e.g. *pāhpisiw* "she chuckles"; e.g. *ē-pāhpisit* "(as) he chuckles"; e.g. *pāhpisināniwan* "there is chuckling"]

pāmwayēs *IPC* before

pās- *VTI* dry s.t. [e.g. *ē-wī-pāsahk* "(as) she is going to dry it"]

pāstē- *VII* be dry, be dried [e.g. *kā-pāstēýik* "that which is dry"]

pē- *IPV* come to, come towards [e.g. *nipē-otihtinik* "she came to grapple me"; e.g. *namōýa wīhkāc ēkotowa nipē-nakiskawāw* "I have never come to meet this kind"; e.g. *ē-pē-nitawāpahtocik* "they came to check up on one another"; e.g. *kā-kī-pē-ay-itahkamikisicik* "what they had been up to"; e.g. *pē-āsē-kīwēw* "he comes back homewards"]

pēht- *VTI* hear s.t. [e.g. *ē-kī-isi-pēhtamān* "(as) I had thus heard"]
pēhtaw- *VTA* hear s.o. [e.g. *kipēhtawāw* "you hear him/her"]
pēkopaýi- *VAI* wake up, wake from sleep [e.g. *ē-pēkopaýicik* "(as) they wake up"]
pēsiw- *VTA* bring s.o. [e.g. *pēsiw* "bring him!"]
pētā- *VAIt* bring s.t. [e.g. *mahti pētā* "please bring it (here)"]
pēyak *IPC* one; a certain one
pēyakwan *IPC* same, the same, just the same
pēyakwāw *IPC* once, at one time
pēyakwāw ēsa *IPH* "once upon at time"; at one time as I am given to understanding [formulaic storytelling opening]
pihkahtēwāpoy- *NI* coffee
pihkohtā- *VAIt* accomplish s.t., achieve s.t., manage to do s.t. [e.g. *ē-isi-pihkohtācik* "(as) they thus managed"]
piko *IPC* only, just; must, have to
piko kīkway *IPH* everything, anything
pimācihāwaso- *VAI* take care of one's children; make a living for one's children [e.g. *ē-pimācihāwasocik* "(as) they make a living for their children"]
pimāciho- *VAI* make a living (from s.t.) [e.g. *ē-kakwē-isi-pimācihocik* "(as) they try to make a living so"]
pimātisi- *VAI* live, be alive, have life [e.g. *ē-pimātisicik* "(as) they live"; e.g. *ta-pimātisiyān* "for me to live"; e.g. *ta-kī-isi-pimātisiyāhk* "how we should live"]
pimi- *IPV* along, in linear progression [e.g. *kā-pim-āyētiskit* "where s/he is leaving tracks"]
pimipahtā- *VAI* run, run along [e.g. *pimipahtāwak* "they run"]
pimipaýi- *VAI* run, travel, drive [e.g. *ē-wī-pimipaýit* "(as) he was going to run"]
pimohtē- *VAI* walk, walk along [e.g. *ē-pa-pimohtēt* "(as) s/he was walking along"]
pimohtēski- *VAI* walk habitually, walk all the time, always walk [habitual; e.g. *kī-pimohtēskiw* "s/he always walked"]
pisiskiw- *NA* animal, wild animal [e.g. *pisiskiwa* "animal (s)[obviative]]

piyak *IPC* one; a certain one [wC; cf. *pēyak*]
piyak kīsikāw *IPH* one day
piyakwāw *IPC* once, at one time [wC; cf. *pēyakwāw*]
piyakwāyihk *IPC* in one spot, on one side [wC; cf. *pēyakwāyihk*]
piýēsīs- *NA* bird, little bird [e.g. *piýēsīsa* "bird(s) [obviative]"]
piýisk *IPC* finally, eventually, at last
pī- *IPV* come to, come towards [wC; cf. *pē-*]
pīhtokwē- *VAI* enter, go inside [e.g. *nitawi-pīhtokwēw* "he goes and enters"]
pīhtokwē-ýahkin- *VTA* push s.o. inside, push s.o. to enter into a house or room [e.g. *kā-pīhtokwē-ýahkināt* "that she pushed him in"]
pīkiskwē- *VAI* speak [e.g. *ta-pīkiskwēyān* "for me to speak; I should speak"]
pīkopit- *VTI* tear s.t. to pieces, rip s.t. apart [e.g. *pīkopitam* "s/he rips it to pieces"]
pīmihtawakēn- *VTA* twist s.o.'s ears, twist s.o. by the ear [e.g. *pāh-pīmihtawakēnēw* "he kept twisting his ears"; *ē-pōni-pīmihtawakēnāt* "(as) he stopped twisting its ears"]
pōni- *IPV* stop, cease [e.g. *ē-pōni-mīcisocik* "(as) they stopped eating"; e.g. *ē-pōni-pīmihtawakēnāt* "(as) he stopped twisting its ears"; e.g. *kā-pōni-wāpahtamāhk* "when we stopped watching it"]
pōni-pimātisi- *VAI* die, cease living [e.g. *pōni-pimātisiw* "he dies"; cf. *pōni- IPV*, *pimātisi- VAI*]
sāh- *IPV* repeatedly, iteratively; augmentative [heavy reduplication of /s/-initial stems; e.g. *sāh-sōhkēpaýihow* "he keeps jumping around vigourously"]
sākahikan- *NI* lake
sākēwē- *VAI* come into view [e.g. *kā-pē-sākēwēt* "he who comes into view"]
sākihito- *VAI* love one another [e.g. *ē-sākihitocik* "(as) they love one another"]
sāmin- *VTI* touch s.t. [e.g. *kā-sāminahk* "that which he touched"]
sāpopatā- *VAIt* wet s.t., make s.t. wet [e.g. *ē-kīsi-sāpopatāt* "(as) she finishes wetting it"]

sēkō- *VAI* go inside, go under, go between (s.t.) [e.g. *sēkōw* "he goes inside"; e.g. *ē-sēkōt* "(as) he goes inside [the mitt]"]

sēmāk *IPC* immediately

sihkos- *NA* weasel [e.g. *sihkosa* "weasel(s) [obviative]"]

sipwēhtahw- *VTA* take s.o. along, leave with s.o. [e.g. *nisipwēhtahwāwak* "I take them along"]

sipwēhtē- *VAI* leave [e.g. *sipwēhtēw* "s/he leaves"; e.g. *pē-sipwēhtēw* "he comes away"]

sīpēkāpitē- *VAI* have clean teeth, have brushed teeth [e.g. *kā-sīpēkāpitēhk* "when teeth are brushed"; cf. *kisīpēkāpitē-*]

sīpēkāpitēho- *VAI* brush one's own teeth [e.g. *ē-kīsi-sīpēkāpitēhoýit* "(as) he [obviative] finishes brushing his own teeth"; cf. *kisīpēkāpitēho-*]

sīpēkāpitēmākwan- *VII* smell like toothpaste; smell like the brushing of teeth [e.g. *kā-sīpēkāpitēmākwahk* "that which smells like toothpaste"; cf. *kisīkāpitēmākwan-*]

sīpēkāpitēwi-pasakwahikan- *NI* toothpaste

sīpēkistikwānē- *VAI* wash one's hair [e.g. *kī-kīsi-sīpēkistikwānēw* "s/he finished washing her/his own hair"; cf. *kisīpēkistikwānē-*]

sīpēkistikwānēn- *VTA* wash s.o.'s hair [e.g. *ka-sīpēkistikwānēnāt* "for her to wash his hair"; cf. *kisīpēkistikwānēn-*]

sīpēkistikwānēniso- *VAI* wash one's own hair [e.g. *ē-sīpēkistikwānēnisot* "(as) she washes her own hair"; e.g. *kī-nitawi-sīpēkistikwānēnisow* "she went to wash his own hair" cf. *kisīpēkistikwānēniso-*]

sīpēkistikwānēwi-sīpēkinikan- *NI* shampoo [cf. *kisīpēkistikwānē- VAI*; *kisīpēkinikan- NI* "soap"]

sōhkēmākwan- *VII* smell strongly; have a strong smell [e.g. *kā-sōhkēmākwahk* "that which has a strong smell"; also: *sōhkimākwan*]

sōhkēpaýiho- *VAI* jump vigourously, throw oneself vigourously [e.g. *sāh-sōhkēpaýihow* "he keeps jumping around vigourously"]

sōniyāw-okimānāhk INM agency, Indian agency [locative; cf. *sōniyāw-okimāw- NA*]

sōniyāw-okimāw- *NA* Indian agent [e.g. locative: *sōniyāw-okimānāhk ohci* "from the agency"] ta- *IPV* to, in order to [marker of conjunct; future infinitival; e.g. *ta-wīkihtot* "for him to be married"; e.g. *ta-sīpēkistikwānēnisot* "for him to wash his own hair"; e.g. *tānisi t-ēsiýihkātisocik* "how they are to be called"; cf. *ka-*]

tahto-kīsikāw *IPC* every day, each day

tahto-pīsim *IPC* every month, each month

tahto-tipiskāw *IPC* every night, each night

tahto-wāpan *IPC* every morning, each day at dawn

tahtw-āskiy *IPC* each year, every year [also: *tahto askiy IPH*]

tahtwāw *IPC* each time, every time

ta-kī- *IPV* should, could, would [modal conjunct marker; e.g. *ta-kī-isi-pimātisiyāhk* "how we should live"; e.g. *ta-kī-isiýihkātisoyēk* "you should call yourselves so"]

takohtatā- *VAIt* arrive with s.t., arrive carrying s.t. [e.g. *ē-takohtatāyān* "(as) I arrive with it"]

takohtē- *VAI* arrive, arrive on foot, arrive walking [e.g. *takohtēw* "he arrives"; e.g. *kā-takohtēcik* "when they arrived"]

takopahtā- *VAI* arrive at a run, arrive running [e.g. *kē-takopahtāt* "he will arrive running"; *kā-pē-takopahtācik* "when they came running back"]

takosin- *VAI* arrive [e.g. *takosin* "s/he arrives"; e.g. *takosihki* "if/when he arrives"]

takwāki-pīsimw- *NA* autumn moon, September [e.g. *takwāki-pīsim*]

tapasī- *VAI* flee, run away [e.g. *nitapasīn* "I flee"]

tāh- *IPV* repeatedly, iteratively; augmentative [heavy reduplication of /t/-initial stems; e.g. *ē-tāh-tāpakwēhk* "(as) snaring is conducted"]

tānimiýikohk *IPC* how much

tānisi *IPC* how, what, in what way; hello, how are you

tānita *IPC* where, where precisely

tānitē *IPC* where, whereabouts

tāpakwamaw- *VTA* snare for s.o., set snares to catch s.o. [e.g. *nitāpakwamawāw* "I set snares to catch him"; e.g. *ē-tāpakwamawācik* "(as) they set snares for it"]

tāpakwān- *NI* snare [e.g. *tāpakwāna* "snare(s) [obviative]"]
tāpakwānis- *NI* snare, small snare [diminutive; cf. *cāpakwānis-*, *tāpakwān-*]
tāpakwāso- *VAI* be snared [e.g. *kā-tāpakwāsot* "which was snared"]
tāpakwāt- *VTA* snare s.o. [e.g. *nika-tāpakwātāw* "I will snare him"]
tāpakwē- *VAI* snare, set snares; set snares for animals [e.g. *ē-tāh-tāpakwēhk* "(as) snaring is conducted; (as) there is snaring"]
tāpiskōc *IPC* like, for instance, as if, just as; it seems that
tāpwē *IPC* truly, really, for sure
tāpwē- *VAI* speak the truth, tell the truth, speak truly [e.g. *ē-tāpwēyān* "(as) I'm telling the truth"; e.g. *ē-tāpwēcik* "(as) they are telling the truth"]
tāpwī *IPC* truly, for sure [wC; cf. *tāpwē IPC*]
tēhtań- *VTA* place s.o. on top [sC; e.g. *kī-tēhtańēwak* "they placed it on top"; cf. pC: *tēhtah-*]
tēhtastā- *VAIt* place s.t. on top [e.g. *kā-kī-tēhtastācik* "where they placed it on top"]
tēpakohp *IPC* seven
tēpihtin- *VII* fit inside, have room to fit in [e.g. *ka-miýo-tēpihtiniýik* "for it [obviative] to fit in well"]
tēpwāt- *VTA* call to s.o.; yell at s.o. [e.g. *ē-matwē-tēpwātāt* "(as) he is calling loudly to her"]
tēsipicikan- *NI* scaffold, burial scaffold; rack, meat rack [e.g. locative: *tēsipicikanihk* "on the scaffold"]
tipiskā- *VII* be night, be dark [e.g. diminutive: *ākwā-cipiskāsin* "it is quite dark"]
tōskin- *VTA* nudge s.o. (i.e. to get his/her attention) [e.g. *ē-tōskināt* "(as) she nudged her (to get her attention)"]
tōtaw- *VTA* do so to s.o.; treat s.o. so [e.g. *tānisi māka ka-tōtawānaw* "but what will we do with it?"]
wahwā *IPC* oh my, my goodness, wow; well!
wahwā hay *IPH* oh my goodness gracious! holy mackerel!
wańawī- *IPV* out, outside [sC: e.g. *ati-wańawī-pa-pakamahwēw* "she pummelled him right outside"; cf. pC: *waýawī-*]
wanikiskisi- *VAI* forget [e.g. *niwanikiskisinān* "we forget"]

wanískā- *VAI* get out of bed, arise from bed, arise from lying; wake up [e.g. *kī-waniskāw* "he arose"; e.g. *ē-waniskācik* "(as) they get up from bed"]
wathawītimihk *IPC* outside, outdoors [wC; cf. pC: *waýawītimihk*]
wawānēýiht- *VTI* be at a loss; fail to think of s.t. [e.g. *wawānēýihtamwak* "they are at a loss"]
wawēsī- *VAI* get dressed up, get dressed in one's best [e.g. *ē-wawēsīt* "(as) he dresses up"]
wawiyatēýihtamaw- *VTA* find it funny for s.o., be amused at it with respect to s.o. [e.g. *ē-wawiyatēýihtamawāyāhkok* "(as) we are amused at them"]
waýawī- *VAI* go outside; go to the bathroom, void [e.g. *ati-waýawīyani* "when you start going outside; when nature starts a'calling"; *kā-waýawīt* "(from where) he voids"]
wā *IPC* well; hey, what?
wācistakāc *IPC* my goodness [exclamation of surprise]
wāhay *IPC* wow! oh my! [exclamation]
wāńaw *IPC* far [sC; cf. pC: *wāhýaw*]
wāpaht- *VTI* see s.t. [e.g. *kā-pōni-wāpahtamāhk* "when we stopped watching it"; e.g. *kā-wāpahtahkik* "that they saw it"]
wāpahtih- *VTA* show (s.t./s.o.) to s.o. [e.g. *ka-nitaw-wāpahtihānaw* "we will go show it to him"; e.g. *wāpahtihēwak* "they show it to him"]
wāpam- *VTA* see s.o. [e.g. *kā-wāpamāt* "they whom s/he saw"; e.g. *namōýa wīhkāc ēkotowa nitōh-wāpamāw* "I have never seen that kind"]
wāpamito- *VAI* see one another [e.g. *kā-kī-wāpamitoyāhk* "when we had seen one another"; cf. *wāpahto-*]
wāpan- *VII* be dawn [e.g. *kē-wāpahk* "when dawn arrives; in the morning"]
wāposw- *NA* rabbit [e.g. *wāpos* "a rabbit"; e.g. *wāposwa* "rabbit(s) [obviative]"; *owāposoma* "his rabbit(s)"; cf. *-wāposom- NDA*]
wāskānipahtā- *VAI* run in a circle; run around an area [e.g. *ka-wāskānipahtānānaw* "we will run in a circle"]
wātiwan- *VII* be a hole, have a hole in it
wāwiyēskońo- *VAI* have a round belly [sC; e.g. *ē-wāwiyēskońot* "(as) he has a rounded belly"]

wēhcitawi *IPC* as usual, as expected [cf. *ohcitaw*]
wiẏa *PrA* he, she; him, her; himself, herself; his, hers [third person singular personal pronoun; cf. sC: *wīńa*, wC: *wītha*]
wiẏawāw *PrA* they, them, themselves; theirs [third person plural personal pronoun; cf. sC: *wīńawāw*, wC: *wīthawāw*]
wiẏisw- *VTA* cut s.o. (animate) out as a pattern; cut a pattern of s.o. [e.g. *wiẏiswēw* "she cuts them out as a pattern"]
wī- *IPV* going to; intend to [prospective aspect; relates the present time period to a future time period; e.g. wC: *namōtha niwī*-Indian*iwin* "I'm not going to be an Indian"; e.g. *kā-kī-wī-itohtēcik* "(where) they were going to go"; e.g. *ē-wī-nātakwēyān* "(as) I'm going to check my snares"; e.g. *kiwī-ka-kociskāsināwāw* "you (all) are going to race against me"; e.g. *wī-asamik* "s/he is going to feed him"]
wīc-āyām- *VTA* live with s.o., cohabit with s.o. [e.g. *ē-wīc-āyāmāt* "(as) he lives with her"]
wīcēwākan- *NDA* his/her companion, partner, friend [third person or unmarked stem form; cf. *-īcēwākan- NDA*]
wīcih- *VTA* help s.o. [e.g. *kī-ohci-wīcihāwak* "they were helped with that"]
wīhkāc *IPC* ever [often in negative constructions, cf. *namōẏa wīhkāc IPH*]
wīhkātaw *IPC* later on [sC]
wīhtamaw- *VTA* tell s.o. s.t., tell s.o. about s.t., tell it to s.o. [e.g. *ē-wīhtamawāt* "(as) she tells her about it"; e.g. *kā-wīhtamawāt* "which he told her"]
wīki *NDI* his/her home, his/her place [third person singular inanimate possessive form; e.g. *wīkiwāhk* "at their home"; cf. -īk- *NDI*]
wīki- *VAI* live, dwell [e.g. *kā-wīkit* "where s/he lives"]
wīkihto- *VAI* be married, get married [e.g. *ē-kī-wīkihtot* "(as) he got married"; *ta-wīkihtot* "for him to marry"]
wīkim- *VTA* marry s.o. [e.g. *ta-wīkimāt* "for him to marry her"; e.g. *kī-wīkimēw* "he married her"]
wīkimākana *NDA* his/her spouse [third person singular animate possessive form; cf. *-īkimākan-* "spouse"]

wīńa *PrA* he, she; him, her; his, hers [sC; third person singular personal pronoun; cf. pC: *wiýa*, sC: *wītha*]

wīnīthimiso- *VAI* have a poor opinion of oneself, think ill of oneself, think of oneself as dirty [wC; e.g. *nikī-wīnīthimisonān* "we had a poor opinion of ourselves"; cf. pC: *wīnēýimiso-*]

wīpac *IPC* early; soon

wīsahkēcāhkw- *NA* Wīsahkēcāhk; trickster, culture hero [e.g. *wīsahkēcāhk*; e.g. *wīsahkēcāhkwa* "Wīsahkēcāhk [obviative]"]

wīsta *PrA* he, too; she, too; him, too; her, too [third person singular emphatic pronoun]

wīstawāw *PrA* they, too; them, too [third person plural emphatic pronoun]

wīth āthisk *IPH* for then, for the reason that [wC; also: *wītha athisk*; cf. *wiý āýisk*, *wiýa aýisk*]

wītha *PrA* he, she; him, her; his, hers [wC; third person singular personal pronoun; cf. pC: *wiýa*; sC: *wīńa*]